MAIGRET AND THE HEADLESS CORPSE

"Profound . . . marvelous . . . the very qualities that make Simenon mysteries a continuing delight."

Book-of-the-Month Club News

THE CLASSIC CRIME COLLECTION

is Avon's highly-acclaimed series of distinguished, suspense novels. Some newly published, some long out of print, all make substantial claim to being standards of the genre. Among authors represented in the series are E. C. Bentley, Philip MacDonald, Hilda Lawrence, Raoul Whitfield, A. A. Milne, C. P. Snow, Vera Caspary, John Dickson Carr, Helen Eustis, Dorothy B. Hughes.

Avon Classic Crime Collection

MAIGRET AND THE HEADLESS CORPSE

Georges Simenon

**Translated from the French
By Eileen Ellenbogen**

A Helen and Kurt Wolff Book

**AVON
CLASSIC CRIME
COLLECTION**

First published in France in 1955 under the title
MAIGRET ET LE CORPS SANS TÊTE.

AVON BOOKS
A division of
The Hearst Corporation
959 Eighth Avenue
New York, New York 10019

First Avon Printing, March, 1971

AVON TRADEMARK REG. U.S. PAT. OFF. AND
FOREIGN COUNTRIES, REGISTERED TRADEMARK—
MARCA REGISTRADA, HECHO EN CHICAGO, U.S.A.

Printed in the U.S.A.

Contents

MAIGRET AND THE HEADLESS CORPSE

Chapter 1

The Fouled
Propeller

In the faint, gray light of early dawn, the barge lay like a shadow on the water. Through the hatchway appeared the head of a man, then shoulders, then the gangling body of Jules, the elder of the two Naud brothers. Running his hands through his tow-colored hair, as yet uncombed, he surveyed the lock, the Quai de Jemmapes to his left, and the Quai de Valmy to his right. In the crisp morning air he rolled a cigarette, and while he was still smoking it a light came on in the little bar on the corner of the Rue des Récollets.

The proprietor, Popaul, came out onto the pavement to take down his shutters. His hair, too, was uncombed, and his shirt open at the neck. In the half-light, the yellow façade of the bar looked more than usually garish.

Rolling his cigarette, Naud came down the gang-plank and across the quay. His brother, Robert, almost as tall and lanky as himself, emerging from below deck in his turn, could see, through the lighted window, Jules leaning on the bar counter and the proprietor pouring a tot of brandy into his coffee.

It was as though Robert were waiting his turn. Exactly as his brother had done, he rolled a cigarette. As the elder brother left the bar, the younger came down the gangplank, so that they met halfway, in the street.

"I'll be starting the engine," said Jules.

Often, in the course of a day, they would not exchange more than a dozen laconic sentences, all relating to their work. They had married twin sisters, and the two families lived on the barge, which was named *The Two Brothers*.

Robert took his elder brother's place at the bar, which smelled of coffee laced with spirits.

"Fine day," said Popaul, who was a tubby little man.

Naud, without a word, glanced out of the window at the sky, which by now was tinged with pink. The slates and tiles of the rooftops and one or two paving stones below were still, after a cold night, coated with a translucent film of rime, which was just beginning to melt here and there. Nothing seemed quite real, except the smoking chimneypots.

The diesel engine spluttered. The exhaust at the rear of the barge spurted black fumes. Naud laid his money on the counter, raised the tips of his fingers to his cap, and returned across the quay. The lockkeeper, in uniform, was at his post, preparing to open the gates. Some way off, on the Quai de Valmy, there were footsteps, but as yet, not another soul in sight. Children's voices could be heard below deck on the barge, where the women were making coffee.

Jules reappeared on deck, leaned over the stern, frowning. His brother could guess what the trouble was. They had taken on a load of gravel at Beauval from Wharf No. 48 on the Ourcq Canal. As usual, they were several tons overweight, and the previous night, as they were drawing away from the dock at La Villette, headed for the Saint-Martin Canal, they had churned up a good deal of mud.

As a rule, in March, there was no shortage of water. This year, however, there had been no rain for two months, and the Canal Authority was hoarding its reserves.

The sluice-gates opened. Jules took the wheel. His brother went ashore to cast off the moorings. The propeller began to turn, and, as they had both feared, thick mud, churned up by the blade, was soon bubbling to the surface. Leaning with all his weight on the boat-hook, Robert tried to head the barge toward the lock. It was as though the propeller were spinning in a vacuum. The lock-keeper, used to this sort of thing, waited patiently, clapping his hands together to keep warm.

The engine shuddered with a grinding sound. Robert looked at his brother, who switched off.

Neither of them could make out what had gone wrong. The propeller, protected by the rudder, could not have scraped the bottom. Something must have got caught in it, a loose cable, maybe, such as is frequently left lying about in canals. If that was the trouble, they were going to have a job disentangling it.

Robert went behind the boat, leaned over, and

felt about in the muddy water with his hook, trying
to reach the propeller. Jules, meanwhile, fetched
a smaller boat-hook. His wife, Laurence, poked her
head through the hatchway.

"What's up?"

"Dunno."

Silently, the two men felt about with their boat-
hooks, trying to reach the fouled propeller. After
a few minutes of this, Dambois the lockkeeper,
known to everyone as Charles, came down to the
quay to watch. He asked no questions, but just
stood by, silently puffing at his pipe, the stem of
which was held together wtih string.

From time to time, people hurried past, office
workers on their way to the Place de la République,
nurses in uniform making for the Hospital of Saint-
Louis.

"Got it?"

"I think so."

"What is it? Rope?"

"I couldn't say."

Jules Naud had certainly hooked something. He
managed, after a time, to free the propeller. Bubbles
rose to the surface.

Gently, hand over hand, he drew up the boat-
hook and, with it, a strange-looking parcel, done up
with string, and a few remnants of sodden newspaper.

It was a human arm, complete from shoulder
to fingertips, which, through long immersion, was
drained white, and limp as a dead fish.

At Police Headquarters, 3rd Division, situated at
the far end of the Quai de Jemmapes, Sergeant
Depoil was just going off night duty when he saw

the lanky figure of the elder Naud standing in the doorway.

"I'm from the barge *The Two Brothers,* up near the lock at the Récollets. We were just pulling out when the propeller jammed. We've fished up a man's arm."

Depoil had served fifteen years in the 10th *Arrondissement*. His first reaction, like that of all the other police officers to be subsequently involved in the case, was incredulity.

"A *man's* arm?" he repeated.

"Yes, a man's. Dark hair on the back of the hand, and . . ."

There was nothing remarkable in the recovery, from the Saint-Martin Canal, of a corpse which had fouled someone's propeller. It had happened before, more than once. But as a rule it was a whole corpse, sometimes that of a man, some old tramp, most likely, who had taken a drop too much and stumbled into the water, or a young thug knifed by someone from a rival gang.

Dismembered bodies were not all that uncommon either. Two or three a year were about average, but invariably, in the Sergeant's long experience, they were women. One knew what to expect right from the start. Nine out of ten would be cheap prostitutes, the kind one sees loitering in lonely places at night.

One could safely conclude, in every case, that the killer was a psychopath.

There was not much one could teach the local police about their neighbors. At the Station, they kept up-to-date records of the activities of every crook, every shady character in the district. Few crimes were committed—from shoplifting to armed robbery—that were not followed in a matter of days by the arrest of the perpetrator. Psychopathic killers, however, were rarely caught.

"Have you brought it with you?" asked Depoil.

"The arm?"

"Where is it?"

"At the quay. Can we go now? There's this load we've got to deliver, Quai de l'Arsenal. They'll be waiting for it."

The Sergeant lit a cigarette and went to the telephone to notify the Salvage Branch. Next, he rang his Divisional Superintendent, Mangrin, at his home.

"Sorry to get you out of bed, sir. A couple of bargees have just fished a human arm out of the canal. No! A man's . . . That's how it struck me too . . . What's that, sir? . . . Yes, he's still here . . . I'll ask him."

Holding the receiver, he turned to Naud:

"Would you say it had been in the water long?"

Jules Naud scratched his head.

"It depends what you mean by long."

"Is it in a very bad state?"

"Hard to tell. Two or three days, I'd say."

The Sergeant repeated into the instrument:

"Two or three days."

Doodling on his notepad, he listened while the Superintendent gave his instructions.

"Can we go?" repeated Naud, when he had hung up.

"Not yet. As the Superintendent quite rightly says, we don't know what else you may have picked up, and if you moved the barge, we might lose it."

"All the same, I can't stop there for ever. There

14

are four others already, lined up to go through the lock. And they're beginning to get impatient."

The Sergeant had dialed another number, and was waiting for a reply.

"Hello! Victor? I hope I haven't waked you. Oh! You're having breakfast, are you? Good. I've got a job for you."

Victor Cadet lived in the Rue du Chemin-Vert, not far from the Police Station, and it was unusual for a month to go by without some call upon his services from that quarter. He had probably retrieved, from the Seine and the canals of Paris, a larger and more peculiar assortment of objects, corpses included, than any other man.

"I'll be with you as soon as I've got hold of my mate."

It was seven o'clock in the morning. In the Boulevard Richard-Lenoir, Madame Maigret, already dressed, as fresh as paint and smelling faintly of soap, was busy in the kitchen getting breakfast. Her husband was still asleep. At the Ouai des Orfèvres, Lucas and Janvier had been on duty since six o'clock. It was Lucas who got the news first.

"There's a queer thing!" he muttered, turning to Janvier, "They've fished an arm out of the Saint-Martin Canal, and it's not a woman's."

"A man's?"

"What else?"

"It could have been a child's."

There had, in fact, been one such case, the only one, three years before.

"What about letting the boss know?"

Lucas looked at the time, hesitated, then shook his head.

"No hurry. He may as well have his coffee in peace."

By ten minutes to eight, a sizable crowd had gathered on the quay where *The Two Brothers* was moored. Anyone trying to get too close to the thing lying on the ground covered with sacking was ordered back by the policeman on guard. Victor Cadet's boat, which had been lying downstream, passed through the lock and came alongside the quay.

Cadet was a giant of a man. Looking at him, one wondered whether his diving suit had had to be made to measure. His mate, in contrast, was undersized and old. He chewed tobacco even on the job, and stained the water with long brown streamers of spittle.

It was he who secured the ladder, primed the pump, and, when everything was ready, screwed on Victor's huge spherical diving helmet.

On deck, near the stern of *The Two Brothers*, could be seen two women and five children, all with hair so fair as to be almost white. One of the women was pregnant, and the other had a baby in her arms.

The buildings of the Quai de Valmy were bathed in sunshine, golden, heart-warming sunshine, which made it hard to credit the sinister reputation of the place. True, there was not much new paint to be seen. The white and yellow façades were streaked and faded. Yet, on this day in March, they looked as fresh as a scene by Utrillo.

There were four barges lined up behind *The Two Brothers*, with washing strung out to dry, and restless children who would not be hushed. A smell of tar mingled with the less agreeable smell of the canal.

At a quarter past eight, Maigret finished his second cup of coffee, wiped his mouth, and was just about to light up his morning pipe when the telephone rang. It was Lucas.

"Did you say a *man's* arm?"

He, too, found it hard to believe.

"Have they found anything else?"

"We've got the diver, Victor, down there now. We'll have to let the barges through fairly soon. There's a bottleneck building up at the lock already."

"Who's on duty there?"

"Judel."

"Inspector Judel, a young policeman of the 10th *Arrondissement,* was conscientious if somewhat dull. He could safely be left in charge at this early stage.

"Will you be going yourself, sir?"

"It's not much out of my way."

"Do you want one of us to meet you there?"

"Who have you got?"

"Janvier, Lemaire . . . Hang on a minute, sir. Lapointe's just come in."

Maigret hesitated. He was enjoying the sunshine. It was warm enough to have the windows open. Was this just a straightforward, routine case? If so, Judel was quite competent to handle it on his own. But at this stage, how could one be sure? If the arm had been a woman's, Maigret would have taken a bet that there was nothing to it.

But since it was a man's arm, anything was possible. And if it should turn out to be a tricky case, and he, the Chief Superintendent, should decide

17

to take over, the day-to-day Headquarters routine would to some extent be affected by his choice of assistant, because, whoever it was, Maigret would want him to see the case through to the end.

"Send Lapointe."

It was quite a while since he had worked in close collaboration with Lapointe. His youth, his eagerness, his artless confusion when he felt he had committed a *faux pas*, amused Maigret.

"Had I better let the Chief know?"

"Yes. I'm sure to be late for the staff meeting."

It was March 23. The day before yesterday had been the first day of spring, and spring was in the air already—which was more than could be said in most years—so much so, in fact, that Maigret very nearly set off without his coat.

In the Boulevard Richard-Lenoir he hailed a taxi. There was no direct bus, and this was not the sort of day for shutting oneself up in the Métro. As he had anticipated, he arrived at the Récollets lock before Lapointe, to find Inspector Judel gazing down into the black waters of the canal.

"Have they found anything else?"

"Not yet, sir. Victor is still working under the barge. There may be something more there."

Ten minutes later, Lapointe drove up in a small black police car, and it was not long before a string of glittering bubbles heralded Victor's return to the surface. His mate hurried forward to unscrew the metal diving helmet. The diver lit a cigarette, looked around, saw Maigret, and greeted him with a friendly wave of the hand.

"Found anything?"

"There's nothing more there."

"Can we let the barge go?"

"It won't turn anything up except mud, that's for sure."

Robert Naud, who had been listening with interest, walked across to his brother.

"Start the engine!"

Maigret turned to Judel.

"Have you got a statement from them?"

"Yes, they've both signed it. Anyway, they'll be at the Quai de l'Arsenal, unloading, for the best part of a week."

The Quai de l'Arsenal was only a couple of miles downstream, between the Bastille and Seine.

The overloaded barge was very low in the water, and it was a slow business getting it away. At last, however, it scraped along the bottom into the lock, and the gates closed behind it.

The crowd of spectators dispersed, leaving only a few idle bystanders who had nothing better to do, and would very likely hang around all day.

Victor was still wearing his diving suit.

"If there's anything else to find," he explained, "it'll be upstream. An arm's light enough to shift with the current, but the rest, legs, torso, head, would sink."

There was not a ripple to be seen on the canal, and floating refuse lay, seemingly motionless, on the surface.

"Of course, there's nothing like the current you get in a river. But each time the level is raised or lowered in the lock, there's movement, though you'd barely notice it, all along the reach."

"In other words, the search ought to extend right up to the next lock?"

"He who pays the piper . . ." said Victor, inhaling and blowing smoke through his nostrils. "It's up to you."

"Will it be a long job?"

"That depends on where we find the rest of the body—assuming, of course, it's in the canal at all."

Why would anyone, getting rid of a body, dump part of it in the canal, and the rest somewhere else— say on some patch of waste ground?

"Carry on."

Cadet signaled to his mate to move the boat a little way upstream, and indicated that he was ready to be screwed into his diving helmet.

Maigret moved away, followed by Judel and Lapointe. They found a solitary little group on the quay, observed by the spectators with the instinctive respect accorded to authority.

"You'll have to search all rubbish dumps and waste ground, of course."

"That's what I thought," said Judel. "I was only waiting for you to give the word."

"How many men can you spare?"

"Two right away. Three by this afternoon."

"Find out if there have been any gang fights or brawls locally in the past few days, and keep your ears open for anyone who may have heard anything —screams, say, or someone shouting for help."

"Very good, sir."

Maigret left the local man on guard over the human arm, which lay covered with sacking on the flagstones of the quay.

"Coming, Lapointe?"

He made for the bar on the corner, with its bright yellow paint, and pushed open the glass door, noting the name, Chez Popaul, inscribed on it. Several local workmen in overalls were having snacks at the counter.

The proprietor hurried forward.

"What can I get you?"

"Do you have a telephone?"

Before the words were out of his mouth, he saw it. It was on the wall next to the bar counter, not enclosed in a booth.

"Come on, Lapointe."

He had no intention of making a phone call where it could be overheard.

"Won't you have something to drink?"

"We'll be back," promised the Chief Superintendent, not wishing to give offense.

Along the quay there were blocks of apartments and concrete office buildings, interpersed with one-story shacks.

"There's bound to be a bistro with a proper telephone booth somewhere around here."

Walking along, they could see, across the canal, the faded flag and blue lamp of the Police Station and, behind it, the dark, massive Hospital of Saint-Louis.

They had gone about three hundred yards when they came to a dingy-looking bar. The Chief Superintendent pushed open the door. Two steps led down into a room with a tiled floor, dark red tiles of the kind commonly seen in Marseilles.

The room was empty except for a large ginger cat lying beside the stove. It got up, stretched lazily, and went out through an open door at the back.

"Anyone there?" called Maigret.

The staccato tick-tock of a cuckoo clock could be heard. The room smelled of spirits and white wine, especially spirits, and there was a faint whiff of coffee.

Someone was moving about in a back room. A woman's voice called out rather wearily, "Coming!"

The ceiling was low and blackened with smoke, and the walls were grimy. Indeed, the whole place was murky, except for faint patches of sunlight here and there. It was like a church lit only by stained-glass windows. A scribbled notice on the wall read: *Snacks served at all hours,* and another: *Patrons are welcome to bring their own food.*

There were, for the time being, no patrons to take advantage of these amenities. It was plain to Maigret and Lapointe that they were the first that day. There was a telephone booth in a corner, but Maigret was waiting for the woman to appear.

When at last she did appear, she shuffled in, sticking pins in her dark, almost black hair. She was thin, sullen-faced, neither young nor old, perhaps in her middle forties. Her felt slippers made no sound on the tiles.

"What do you want?"

Maigret and Lapointe exchanged glances.

"Have you a good white wine?"

She shrugged.

"Two white wines. And a *jeton* for the phone."

He went into the telephone booth, shutting the door behind him, and rang the Public Prosecutor's office to make his report. The Deputy to whom he spoke was as surprised as everyone else to hear that the arm fished out of the canal was a man's.

"The diver is working upstream now. He says if there's anything more to find, that's where it will be. The next step, as far as I'm concerned, is to have Doctor Paul examine the arm as soon as possible."

"I'll get in touch with him at once and call you back, if that suits you."

Maigret, having read out the number on the dial, went over to the bar. Two glasses of wine stood ready poured on the counter.

"Your very good health," he said, raising his glass to the woman.

For all the interest she showed, he might not have spoken. She just stared vacantly, waiting for them to go, so that she might finish making herself presentable, or whatever it was she had been doing when they arrived.

She must have been attractive, once. She had, like everyone else, undoubtedly once been young. Now, everything about her eyes, her mouth, her whole body, was listless, faded. Was she a sick woman, anticipating a dreaded attack? Sometimes sick people who knew that, at a particular hour of the day, the pain would recur, wore that same look of apathy mixed with apprehension, like drug addicts in need of a shot.

"They're calling me back," murmured Maigret, sounding apologetic.

It was, of course, like any other bar or café, a public place, impersonal in a sense, yet both men had the feeling of being intruders who had blundered in where they had no right to be.

"Your wine is very good."

It really was good. Most Paris bistros advertise a *petit vin du pays,* but this, as a rule, turns out to be a wholesale product, straight from Bercy. This wine was different. It had a distinctive regional

23

flavor, though the Superintendent could not quite place it.

"Sancerre?" he ventured.

"No. It comes from a little village near Poitiers."

That accounted for the slight flinty tang.

"Is that where you come from?"

She did not answer. She just stood there, motionless, silent, impassive. Maigret was impressed. The cat, which had come into the room with her, was rubbing its back against her bare legs.

"What about your husband?"

"He's gone there to get more."

More wine, she meant. Making conversation with her was far from easy. The Superintendent had just signaled to her to refill the glasses when, much to his relief, the telephone rang.

"Yes, it's me. Did you get hold of Paul? When will he be free? An hour from now? Right, I'll be there."

The Deputy talked. Maigret listened in silence, with an expression of deepening disapproval, as it sank in that the Examining Magistrate in charge of the case was to be Judge Coméliau. He was the most pettifogging, niggling man on the Bench, and Maigret's very own private and personal enemy.

"He says, will you please see to it that he's kept in the picture."

"I know."

Maigret knew all too well what he was in for: five or six phone calls a day from Coméliau, not to mention a briefing session every morning in the magistrate's office.

"Ah, well," he sighed, "we'll do our best."

"Don't blame me, Superintendent. There just wasn't anyone else available."

The sunlight had penetrated a little farther into the room, and just reached Maigret's glass.

"Let's go," he said, feeling in his pocket for change. "How much?"

And, outside in the street:

"Have you got the car?"

"Yes, I left it over by the lock."

The wine had put color in Lapointe's cheeks, and his eyes were bright. From where they were, they could see a little group of onlookers watching the driver's progress from the edge of the quay. As Maigret and the Inspector came up to them, Victor's mate pointed to a bundle in the bottom of the boat. It was larger than the first.

"A leg and foot," he called out, and spat into the water. This time, the wrapping was in quite good condition. Maigret saw no necessity to take a closer look.

"Shall we need a hearse?" he asked Lapointe.

"There's plenty of room in the trunk, of course."

The prospect did not commend itself to either of them, but they did have an appointment at the Forensic Laboratory, a large, bright, modern building overlooking the Seine, not far from the junction of the river and the canal. It would not do to keep the pathologist waiting.

"What should I do?" Lapointe asked.

Maigret could not bring himself to say. Repressing his revulsion, Lapointe carried the two bundles, one after the other, to the car, and laid them in the trunk.

"Do they smell?" asked the Superintendent, when Lapointe rejoined him at the water's edge.

Lapointe, who was holding his hands out in front of him, nodded, wrinkling his nose.

Doctor Paul, in white overall and rubber gloves, smoked incessantly. He subscribed to the theory that there was no disinfectant like tobacco, and often, during a single autopsy, would smoke as many as two packs of Bleues Gauloises.

He worked briskly and cheerfully, bent over the marble slab, chatting between puffs.

"Naturally, I can't say anything definite at this stage. For one thing, there's not a great deal to learn from a leg and an arm on their own. The sooner you find the rest of the body, the better. Meanwhile, I'll do as many tests as I can."

"What age would you say?"

"As far as I can tell at a glance, a man somewhere between fifty and sixty—nearer fifty than sixty. Take a look at this hand."

"What about it?"

"It's a broad, strong hand, and it's done rough work in its time."

"A laborer?"

"No. A farm worker, more likely. Still, it's a fair bet that that hand hasn't gripped a heavy implement for years. This was not a fastidious man. You can tell by the nails, especially the toenails."

"A tramp?"

"I don't think so, but, as I say, I can't be sure till I have more to go on."

"Has he been dead long?"

"Again, I can only hazard a guess—don't take my word for it. I may have changed my mind by tonight or tomorrow. But, for the time being, I'm fairly confident that he died not more than three days ago, at the very outside."

"Not last night?"

"No, the night before that, possibly."

Maigret and Lapointe were smoking too, and, as far as they could, they kept their eyes averted from the marble slab. As for Doctor Paul, he seemed to be enjoying his work, handling his instruments like a juggler.

He was changing into his outdoor clothes when Maigret was called to the telephone. It was Judel from the Quai de Valmy.

"They've found the torso!" he announced, sounding quite excited about it.

"No head?"

"Not yet. According to Victor, it won't be so easy. Because of its weight, it will probably be sunk in the mud. He's found an empty wallet and a woman's handbag, though."

"Near the torso?"

"No, quite a long way off. There probably isn't any connection. As he says, every time he goes down, he finds enough junk to open a stall in the Flea Market. Just before he found the torso, he came up with a child's cot and a couple of slop pails."

Paul, holding his hands out in front of him, was waiting before taking off his gloves.

"Any news?" he asked.

Maigret nodded. Then to Judel:

"Can you get it to me at the Forensic Lab?"

"I'm sure we can manage it."

"Right. I'll be here, but be quick about it, because Doctor Paul . . ."

They waited outside the building, enjoying the fresh air, and watching the flow of traffic on the Pont d'Austerlitz. Across the Seine, several barges and a small sailing boat were unloading at the quayside opposite a warehouse. Paris, in the morning sun, was throbbing with youth and gaiety. It was the first real spring day. Life was full of promise.

"No tattoo marks or scars, I suppose?"

"None on the arm or leg, at any rate. From the condition of the skin, I'd say he was not an outdoor type."

"Hairy, though."

"Yes. I have a fair idea of what he must have looked like. Dark, broad-shouldered, but below medium height, with well-developed muscles, and coarse dark hair on the arms, hands, legs, and chest. A real son of the soil, sturdy, independent, stubborn. The countryside of France is full of men like him. It'll be interesting to see his head."

"If we ever find it!"

A quarter of an hour later, two uniformed policemen arrived with the torso. Doctor Paul, all but rubbing his hands, got to work at the marble slab like a craftsman at his bench.

"As I thought," he grumbled. "This isn't a skilled job. What I mean to say is: this man wasn't dismembered by a butcher or a Jack-the-Ripper, still less by a surgeon! The joints were severed by an ordinary hack-saw. The rest of the job, I'd say, was done with a large carving knife. All restaurants have them, and most private kitchens. It must have been a longish job. It couldn't have been done all at once.

He paused.

"Take a look at this chest. What do you see, and I don't mean hair?"

Maigret and Lapointe glanced at the torso, and looked away quickly.

"No visible scars?"

"I don't see any. I'm certain of one thing. Drowning wasn't the cause of death."

It was almost comical. How on earth would a man found in pieces in a canal contrive to drown?

"I'll examine the organs next, and especially—in so far as it's practicable—the contents of the stomach. Will you be staying?"

Maigret shook his head. He had seen quite enough. He could hardly wait to get to a bar and have a drink, not wine this time, but a drop of the hard stuff, to get rid of the foul taste in his mouth, which seemed to him like the taste of death.

"Just a minute, Maigret. What was I saying? D'you see this white line here, and these small white spots on the abdomen?"

The Superintendent nodded, but did not look.

"That's an old operation scar. Quite a few years old. Appendectomy."

"And the spots?"

"Now there's an odd thing. I couldn't swear to it, but I'm almost sure they're grapeshot or buckshot wounds, which confirms my feeling that the man must have lived in the country at some time or other. A small farmer or gamekeeper, maybe. Who knows? A long time ago, twenty years or more, someone must have emptied a shotgun into him. There are seven, no, eight of these scars in a curve, like a rainbow. Only once before in the whole of my life have I ever seen anything like them, and they weren't so evenly spaced. I'll have to photograph them for the record."

"Will you give me a ring?"

"Where will you be? At the Quai des Orfèvres?"

"Yes. In my office, and I'll probably lunch in the Place Dauphine."

"As soon as I have anything to report, I'll let you know."

Maigret led the way out into the sunshine and mopped his forehead. Lapointe felt impelled to spit several times into the gutter. He, too, it seemed, had a bitter taste in his mouth.

"As soon as we get back to Headquarters, I'll have the trunk fumigated," he said.

On their way to the car park, they went into a bistro for a glass of marc brandy. It was so potent that Lapointe retched, held his hand to his mouth, and, for a moment, with eyes watering, wondered anxiously whether he was going to be sick.

When he felt better, he muttered:

"Sorry about that."

As they went out, the proprietor of the bar remarked to one of the customers:

"That's another of them come from identifying a corpse. It always makes them that way."

Situated as he was, directly opposite the mortuary, he was used to it.

Chapter 2

Red
Sealing Wax

When Maigret came into the great central lobby of
the Quai des Orfèvres he was, for a second or two,
dazzled, because even this lobby, surely the grayest
and dingiest place on earth, was sunlit today, or at
least gilded with luminous dust.

On the benches between the office doors, there
were people waiting, some handcuffed. As Maigret
went past, to report to the Chief of Police on the
Quai de Valmy case, a man stood up and touched
his hat in greeting.

With the familiarity born of daily meetings over
many years, Maigret called out:

"Well, Vicomte, what have you got to say for
yourself? You can't complain this time that it's just
another case of someone chopping up a whore."

The man known to everyone as the Vicomte did
not seem to object to his nickname, although he
must have been aware of the innuendo. He was, in

a discreet way, a homosexual. For the past fifteen years he had "covered" the Quai des Orfèvres for a Paris newspaper, a press agency, and some twenty provincial dailies.

In appearance, he was the last of the Boulevard dandies, dressed with Edwardian elegance, wearing a monocle on a black ribbon around his neck. Indeed, it could well have been the monocle (which he hardly ever used) that had earned him his nickname.

"Have they found the head?"

"Not to my knowledge."

"I've just spoken to Judel on the phone. He says, no. If you get any fresh news, Superintendent, don't forget me."

He returned to his bench, and Maigret went into the Chief's office.

The window was open, and from there, too, one could see river craft plying up and down the Seine. The two men engaged in pleasant conversation for ten minutes or so.

The first thing Maigret saw when he went through the door of his own office was a note on his blotting pad. He knew at once what it was—a message from Judge Coméliau, of course, asking him to phone him as soon as he got in.

"Chief Superintendent Maigret here, Judge."

"Ah! Good morning, Maigret. Are you just back from the canal?"

"From the Forensic Lab."

"Is Doctor Paul still there?"

"He's working on the internal organs now."

"I take it the corpse hasn't been identified yet?"

"With no head, there's not much hope of that. Not unless we have a stroke of luck . . ."

"That's the very thing I wanted to discuss with you. In a straightforward case, where the identity of the victim is known, one can tell more or less where one is going. Do you follow me? Now, in this case, we haven't the faintest idea who may be involved. Within the next hour, or the next day or two, we may be in for a nasty shock. We must be prepared for the worst, the very worst, and therefore would do well to proceed with extreme caution."

Coméliau enunciated every syllable, and liked the sound of his own voice. Everything he said or did was of "extreme" importance.

Most examining magistrates were content to leave matters in the hands of the police until they had completed their inquiries. Not so Coméliau. He always insisted on directing operations from the outset, owing, no doubt, to his exaggerated dread of "complications." His brother-in-law was an ambitious politician, one of a handful of Deputies with a finger in every departmental pie. Coméliau was fond of saying:

"You must understand that, owing to his position, I am more vulnerable than my brother-magistrates."

Maigret got rid of him eventually by promising to inform him immediately of any new development, however trivial, even if it meant disturbing him at his home in the evening. He looked through his mail, and then went to the Inspectors' Duty Room, to give them their orders for the day.

"Today is Tuesday, isn't it?"

"That's right, sir."

If Doctor Paul has estimated correctly that the body had been in the Saint-Martin Canal about forty-eight hours, then the crime must have been committed on Sunday, almost certainly during the evening or night, since it was hardly likely that anyone intent on getting rid of a number of bulky and sinister packages would be so foolhardy as to attempt it in broad daylight with the Police Station not five hundred yards away.

"Is that you, Madame Maigret?" he said playfully to his wife, when he had got her on the line. "I shan't be home for lunch. What were we having?"

Haricot mutton. He had no regrets. Too stodgy for a day like this.

He rang Judel.

"What news?"

"Victor is having a snack in the boat. The whole body has been recovered, except the head. He wants to know if he's to go on looking."

"Of course."

"I've got my men on the job, but they haven't come up with anything much so far. There was a bit of trouble in a bar on the Rue des Récollets on Sunday night. Not Chez Popaul. Father up towards the Faubourg Saint-Martin. A concierge has reported the disappearance of her husband, but he's been missing for over a month, and the description doesn't fit."

"I'll probably be along sometime this afternoon."

On his way to lunch at the Brasserie Dauphine, he looked in at the Inspectors' Duty Room.

"Ready, Lapointe?"

He really did not need his young assistant just to share the table at which he always sat in the little restaurant in the Place Dauphine. This thought struck him as they walked along in companionable silence. He smiled to himself, remembering a question that had once been put to him on this subject. His friend, Doctor Pardon of Rue Popincourt, with whom he and his wife dined regularly once a month, had turned to him one evening and asked very earnestly:

"Can you explain to me, Maigret, why it is that plainclothes policemen, like plumbers, always go about in pairs?"

He had never thought about it, though on reflection he had to admit that it was a fact. He himself, when he was out on a case, almost always took an inspector with him.

He had scratched his head.

"I imagine it goes back to the days when Paris was a lawless city, and it wasn't safe to go into some districts alone, especially at night."

It was not safe even today to make an arrest singlehanded, or venture into the underworld on one's own. But the more Maigret had thought about it, the less this explanation had satisfied him.

"And another thing. Take a suspect who has reluctantly made some damaging admission, either in his own home or at Headquarters. If there had been only one police officer present at the time, it would be that much easier to deny everything later. And a jury will always attach more weight to evidence when there is a witness to corroborate it."

All very true, but still not the whole truth.

"Then there's the practical angle. Say someone is being shadowed. Well, you can't watch him like a hawk and make a telephone call at the same time. And then again, more often than not, your quarry will go into a building with several exits."

35

Pardon had smiled then as Maigret was smiling now.

"I'm always suspicious," he said, "of tortuous answers to simple questions."

To which Maigret had retorted:

"Well, then, speaking for myself, I usually take an inspector along for company. I'm afraid I'd be bored stiff on my own."

He did not repeat this conversation to Lapointe. One should never poke fun at the illusions of youth, and the sacred fire still burned in Lapointe. It was pleasant and peaceful in the little restaurant, with other police officers dropping in for a drink at the bar, and four or five lunching in the dining room.

"Will the head be found in the canal, do you think?"

Maigret, rather to his own surprise, shook his head. To be honest, he had not given the matter much thought. His response had been instinctive. He could not have said why he just had a feeling that the diver, Victor, would find nothing more in the mud of the Saint-Martin Canal.

"Where can it be?"

He had no idea. In a suitcase at a baggage checkroom, maybe. At the Gare de l'Est, a few hunderd yards from the canal, or the Gare du Nord, not much farther away. Or it might have been sent by road to some address or other in the provinces, in one of the fleet of heavy, long-distance trucks that the Superintendent had seen lined up in a side street off the Quai de Valmy. These particular trucks were red and green, and Maigret had often seen them about the streets, heading for the highways. Until today, he had had no idea where their depot was. It was right there in the Rue Terrage, next to the canal. At one time during the morning he had noticed twenty or more of them strung out along the road, all inscribed: "Zenith Transport. Roulers and Langlois."

When Maigret directed his attention to details of this kind, it usually meant that he was thinking of nothing in particular. The case was interesting enough, but not absorbing. What interested him more, at the moment, was the canal itself and its surroundings. At one time, right at the beginning of his career, he had been familiar with every street in this district, and could have identified many a night prowler who slunk past in the shadow of the buildings.

They were still sitting over their coffee when Maigret was called to the telephone. It was Judel.

"I was in two minds about calling you, sir. I wouldn't exactly call it a lead, but one of my men, Blancpain, thinks he may be on to something. I posted him near where the driver is working, and about an hour ago his attention was attracted by an errand boy on a delivery bicycle. He had a feeling he'd seen him before, earlier, more than once, at regular intervals of about half an hour, in fact. People have been coming to the quay all day to watch the diver. Most of them stay for a bit and then wander away, but this character, according to Blancpain, kept to himself, and seemed to be drawn there by something more than curiosity. Errand boys, as a rule, work to a pretty tight schedule on their rounds, and don't have all that much time to waste."

"Has Blancpain spoken to him?"

"He was intending to, but as soon as he made a move toward him—very casually, so as not to scare him off—the boy hopped onto his bicycle and pedaled away at top speed toward the Rue des Récollets. Blancpain did chase after him, but couldn't make much headway in a crowded street on foot—he had no transport—and finally lost him in the traffic of the Faubourg Saint-Martin."

There was a brief silence. It was all very vague, of course. It might mean nothing. On the other hand, it could be a breakthrough.

"Was Blancpain able to describe him?"

"Yes. A fellow of between eighteen and twenty— probably a country boy—very healthy complexion —fair—longish hair—wearing a leather jacket and a turtle-neck sweater. Blancpain couldn't read the name of the firm on his bicycle, but he was able to see that one word ended in 'ail.' We're checking on all the local shopkeepers who employ an errand boy."

"What news from Victor?"

"He says that as long as he's getting paid for it, he doesn't care whether he's under water or on dry land, but he's sure it's a waste of time."

"What about the rubbish dumps and waste ground?"

"Nothing so far."

"I should be getting the pathologist's report shortly. I'm hoping that will tell us something about the dead man."

At half past two, when Maigret was back in his office, Paul rang to report his findings, which would later be confirmed in writing.

"Do you want it at dictation speed, Maigret?"

Maigret drew a writing pad toward him.

"I've had to rely on guesswork to some extent, but I think you'll find I'm not far out. First of all, here's a description of your man as far as one can be certain in the absence of the head. Not very tall, about five foot eight. Short, thick neck and, I feel sure, round face and heavy jowl. Dark hair, possibly graying a little at the temples. Weight: a hundred an sixty-seven pounds. I would describe him as thickset, stock rather than tubby, muscular rather than fat, though he did put on a bit of weight toward the end. The condition of the liver suggests a steady drinker, but I wouldn't say he was an alcoholic. More probably the sort who likes a glass of something, white wine mostly, every hour or even every half-hour. I did, in fact, find traces of white wine in the stomach."

"Any food?"

"Yes. It was lucky for us that his last meal— lunch or dinner, whichever it was—was indigestible. It consisted mainly of roast pork and haricot beans."

"How long before he died?"

"Two to two and a half hours, I'd say. I've sent scrapings from under his toenails and fingernails to the laboratory. Moers will be getting in touch with you direct about them."

"What about the scars?"

"I can confirm what I told you this morning. The appendectomy was performed five or six years ago, by a good surgeon, judging from the quality of the work. The buckshot scars are at least twenty years old, and if you ask me, I'd say nearer forty."

"Age?"

"Fifty to fifty-five."

"Then he would have got the buckshot wound as a child?"

"In my opinion, yes. General health satisfactory,

39

apart from the inflammation of the liver that I've already mentioned. Heart and lungs in good condition. There's a very old tuberculosis scar on the left lung, but it doesn't mean much. It's quite common for babies and young children to contract a mild form of TB which no one even notices. Well, that's about it, Maigret. If you want any more information, bring me the head, and I'll do my best to oblige."

"We haven't found it yet."

"In that case, you never will."

There, Maigret agreed with him. There are some beliefs in the Quai des Orfèvres which have been held so long that they have come to be taken for granted. The belief, for instance, that, as a general rule, only the corpses of cheap prostitutes are found dismembered. And the belief that, although the torso is usually found, the head is not.

No one questions these beliefs, they are just accepted by everyone.

Maigret stumped off to the Inspectors' Duty Room.

"If I'm wanted, I'll be upstairs in the lab."

He climbed slowly to the top floor of the Palais de Justice, where he found Moers poring over his test tubes.

"Is that my corpse you're working on?" he asked.

"I'm analyzing the specimens Paul sent up to us."

"Found anything?"

The laboratory was immense, and full of pathologists absorbed in their work. Standing in one corner was the dummy used in the reconstruction of crimes, for instance, in a case of stabbing, to determine the relative positions of victim and assailant.

"It's my impression," murmured Moers, who always spoke in a whisper, as though he were in church, "that your man seldom went out of doors."

"What makes you think that?"

"I've been examining the particles of matter taken from under his toenails. That's how I can tell you that the last pair or socks he wore were navy-blue wool. I also found traces of the kind of felt used for making carpet slippers, from which I conclude that the man practically lived in his slippers."

"If you're right, Paul should be able to confirm it, because if one lives in slippers over a long period, one ends up with deformed feet, or so my wife always tells me, and . . ." He broke off in mid-sentence to telephone Doctor Paul at the Forensic Laboratory. Finding that he had already left, he rang his home.

"Maigret here. Just one question, Doctor. It's Moers's idea really. Did you get the impression that our man wore carpet slippers most of the time?"

"Good for Moers! I almost said as much to you earlier, but it was just an impression, and I didn't want to set you on a false trail. It came into my mind, while I was examining the feet, that the man might have worked in a café or a bar. Barmen, like waiters and policemen—especially policemen on traffic duty—tend to get fallen arches, not because they do much walking, but because they stand for long hours."

"You mentioned that the fingernails were not well kept."

"That's true. It's not very likely that a hotel waiter would have black fingernails."

"Nor a waiter in a large brasserie or a respectable café."

41

"Has Moers found anything else?"

"Not so far. Many thanks, Doctor."

Maigret stayed in the laboratory for almost an hour, roaming about, and leaning over the benches to watch the technicians at their work.

"Would it interest you to know that there were also traces of soil mixed with potassium nitrate under the nails?"

Moers knew as well as Maigret where such a mixture was most often to be found: in a cellar, especially a damp cellar.

"Was there much of it?"

"That's what struck me. This was ingrained, occupational dirt."

"In other words, a man who regularly worked in a cellar?"

"That would be my guess."

"What about the hands?"

"There are traces of the same mixture under the fingernails, and other things too, including minute splinters of red sealing wax."

"The kind used for sealing wine bottles?"

"Yes."

Maigret was almost disappointed. It was beginning to look too easy.

"In other words, a bistro!" he muttered grumpily.

Just then, in fact, it seemed to him more than likely that the case would be over that same evening. He saw, in his mind's eye, the thin, dark woman who had served him with a drink that morning. She had made a deep impression on him, and she had been in his mind more than once that day, not necessarily because he had associated her with the dismembered man, but because he had recognized her as someone out of the ordinary.

There was no lack of colorful characters in a district such as the Quai de Valmy. But he had seldom come across anyone as negative as this woman. It was hard to put it into words. As a rule, when two people look at one another, an interchange of some sort, however slight, takes place. A relationship is established, if only a hostile one.

Not so with this woman. Her face, when she had seen them standing at the bar, had betrayed no trace of surprise or fear, no trace of anything, indeed, but a profound and seemingly habitual lassitude.

Or was it indifference?

Two or three times, between sips of wine, Maigret had looked her straight in the eye, but there had been no response, not so much as the flicker of an eyelash.

Yet it was not the insensibility of a moron. Nor was she drunk or drugged, at least not at that moment. He had made up his mind there and then that he would pay her another visit, if only to discover what kind of people her customers were.

"Are you on to something, sir?"

"Maybe."

"You don't sound exactly overjoyed."

Maigret did not care to pursue the subject. At four o'clock he went in search of Lapointe, who was catching up on his paper-work.

"Would you mind driving me over there?"

"To the canal?"

"Yes."

"I hope they'll have had time to fumigate the car."

There were brightly colored hats in the streets already, with red this year as the dominant color,

43

brilliant poppy-red. The awnings, plain orange or candy-striped, were down over the street cafés. There were people at almost every table, and there seemed to be a new air of cheerful briskness about the passers-by.

At the Quai de Valmy, a small crowd was gathered near where Victor was still searching the bed of the canal. Among them was Jubel. Maigret and Lapointe got out of the car and went over to him.

"Nothing more?"

"No."

"No clothing?"

"We've been working on the string. If you think it would help, I'll send it up to the lab. As far as we can tell, it's just the ordinary coarse string most shopkeepers use. Quite a lot was needed for all those parcels. I've got someone making inquiries in the local hardware shops, so far without results. Then there's what's left of the newspapers that were used for wrapping. I've had them dried out, and they're mostly last week's."

"What's the most recent date?"

"Saturday morning."

"Do you know that bistro in the street just beyond the Rue Terrage, the one next door to the surgical instruments place?"

"Chez Calas?"

"I didn't notice the name; it's a murky little place below street level, with a big charcoal stove in the middle, and a zinc bar counter painted black, stretching almost from end to end."

"That's it. Omer Calas's place."

When it came to local landmarks, the district police had the edge on the Quai des Orfèvres.

"What sort of place is it?" asked Maigret, watching the air bubbles which marked Victor's coming and going under water.

"Quiet. They've never given us any trouble, as far as I know."

"Would you say Omer Calas was a townsman or a countryman?"

"A countryman, I should think. I could look up his registration. It's always happening. A man comes to Paris as a personal servant or chauffeur, and ends up married to the cook and running a bistro in double harness."

"Have they been there long?"

"Longer than I have. As far back as I can remember, it's always been much the same. It's almost opposite the Police Station, and I occasionally drop in for a drink. They have a good white wine."

"Who looks after the bar? The proprietor?"

"Most of the time—except for an hour or two every afternoon, when he's at a brasserie in the Rue La Fayette playing billiards. He's keen on billiards."

"When he's away, does the woman look after the bar?"

"Yes, they have no staff. I seem to remember they did have a little waitress at one time, but I've no idea what became of her."

"What sort of people go there?"

"It's hard to say," said Judel, scratching the back of his head.

"All the bistros hereabouts cater to more or less the same class of customer, and yet no two are alike. Take Chez Popaul, opposite the lock. It's busy from morning to night. There it's neat spirits and rowdy talk, and there's always a blue haze of tobacco smoke about the place. Any time after eight at night you're sure to find three or four women in there, waiting for their regular fellows."

"And Omer's place?"

"Well, for one thing it's a bit off the beaten track, and for another, it's dark and rather gloomy. You must have noticed the atmosphere yourself. They get dockers from thereabouts dropping in for a drink in the morning, and a few take their sandwiches along at lunchtime, and order a glass of white wine. There's not much doing in the afternoon, and I daresay that's why Omer goes off for his game of billiards after lunch. As I said, there are no regulars at that time, just the occasional passer-by. Trade picks up again at the end of the day.

"I've been in myself once or twice of an evening. It's always the same. A hand of cards at one of the tables, and a couple of people, no more, drinking at the bar. It's one of those joints where, if one doesn't happen to be a regular, one is made to feel out of place."

"Is the woman Omer's wife?"

"I've never thought to ask. I can easily find out, though. We can go over to the station now, if you'd like, and look them up in the records."

"I'll leave that to you. You can let me know later. Omar Calas is away from home, it seems."

"Oh? Is that what she told you?"

"Yes."

By now, the Naud brothers' barge had docked at the Quai de l'Arsenal, and the cargo of gravel was being unloaded by crane.

"I should be grateful if you would compile a list of all the bistros in the district, drawing my atten-

46

tion to any whose proprietor or barman has been
absent since Sunday."

"Do you think . . . ?"

"It's Moers's idea. He may be right. I'm going
along there."

"To Calas's?"

"Yes. Coming, Lapointe?"

"Shall we be needing Victor tomorrow?"

"We can't chuck the taxpayer's money out of the
window. I have a feeling that, if there had been
anything more to find, he'd have found it today."

"That's what he thinks, too."

"Tell him he can give up as soon as he feels like
it, and not to forget to let me have his report by
tomorrow."

Maigret paused on his way, to take another look
at the trucks in the Rue Terrage, and read the in-
scription, "Roulers and Langlois," over the great
archway of the depot.

"I wonder how many there are," he murmured,
thinking aloud.

"What?" Lapointe asked.

"Trucks."

"I've never driven into the country without finding myself crawling along behind one. It's damned
near impossible to pass them."

The chimneypots, which had been rose-pink that
morning, were now a deepening red in the setting
sun, and there were pale green streaks here and
there in the sky, green streaks almost the same
color as the green sea at dusk.

"Do you really believe, sir, that a woman could
have done it?"

He thought again of the thin, dark woman who
had poured their drinks that morning.

47

"It's possible . . . I don't know."

Perhaps Lapointe felt, as he did, that it was all too easy.

Confront the men of the Quai des Orfèvres with a thoroughly tangled and apparently insoluble problem, and you will have every one of them, Maigret most of all, fretting and grumbling over it. But give them something that, at first sight, seems difficult, and later turns out to be straightforward and commonplace, and those same men, Maigret included, will not be able to contain their disappointment.

They were at the door of the bistro. On account of its low ceiling, it was darker than most, and there was already a light switched on over the counter.

The same woman, carelessly dressed as she had been in the morning, was serving two men, office workers by the look of them. She must have recognized Maigret and his colleague, but she showed no sign of it.

"What will you have?" was all she said, without so much as a smile.

"White wine."

There were three or four bottles with drawn corks in a bucket behind the counter. Presumably it was necessary to go down to the cellar from time ot time to get more. The floor behind the bar was not tiled, and there was a trap door, about three foot square, leading, no doubt, to the cellar below. Maigret and Lapointe had not taken their drinks to a table. From the conversation of the two men standing beside them at the bar, they gathered that they were not, in fact, office workers, but male nurses on night shift at the Hospital of Saint-Louis on the other side of the canal. From something one of them said to the woman, it was evident that they were regulars.

"When do you expect Omer back?"

"You know he never tells me anything."

She replied un-self-consciously, and with the same indifference as she had shown when Maigret had spoken to her earlier in the day. The ginger cat was still stretched out beside the stove, with every appearance of having been there all day.

"I hear they're still searching for the head!" said the man who had asked about her husband. As he spoke, he glanced at Maigret and his companion. Had he seen them on the quay earlier in the day? Or was it just that he could tell by the look of them that they were policemen?

"It hasn't been found, has it?" he went on, addressing himself direct to Maigret.

"Not yet."

"Do you think it will be found?"

The other man subjected Maigret to a long stare, and then said:

"You're Chief Superintendent Maigret, aren't you?"

"Yes."

"I thought so. I've often seen your picture in the papers."

The woman still did not bat an eyelid. For all one could tell, she had not even heard.

"It's weird, carving up a man like that! Coming, Julien? How much, Madame Calas?"

With a slight nod to Maigret and Lapointe, they went out.

"Do you get many of the hospital staff in here?"

"A few."

She did not waste words.

"Has your husband been away since Sunday?"

She looked at him blankly and asked, as though it were a matter of indifference to her:

"Why Sunday?"

"I don't know. I thought I heard . . ."

"He left on Friday afternoon."

"Were there many people in the bar then?"

She seemed to be trying to remember. At times, she looked so withdrawn—or bored, was it?—that she might have been a sleepwalker.

"There are never many people in the afternoon."

"Was there anyone at all? Try and think."

"There may have been. I don't remember. I didn't notice."

"Did he have any luggage?"

"Of course."

"Much?"

"A suitcase."

"What was he wearing?"

"A gray suit. I think. Yes."

"Do you know where he is now?"

"No."

"Didn't he say where he was going?"

"I know he must have taken the train to Poitiers. From there, he'll have gone on by bus to Saint-Aubin or some other village in the district."

"Does he stay at the local inn?"

"As a rule."

"Doesn't he ever stay with friends or relatives? Or on one of the estates where he gets his wine?"

"I've never asked him."

"You mean to say that if you needed to get in touch with him urgently, to pass on some important message, for instance, or because you were ill, you wouldn't know where to find him?"

This too appeared to be a matter of indifference to her.

"Sooner or later he'd be bound to come back," she said in her flat, monotonous voice. "The same again?"

Both glasses were empty. She refilled them.

Chapter 3

The Errand
Boy

It was, all in all, one of Maigret's most frustrating interrogations. Not that one could call it an interrogation in the accepted sense, with life going on as usual around them. The Chief Superintendent and Lapointe stood at the bar for a long time, sipping their drinks like ordinary customers. And that was what they really were. True, one of the male nurses had recognized Maigret earlier, and had addressed him by name, but the Superintendent, when speaking to Madame Calas, made no reference to his official standing. He would ask a question. She would reply, briefly. Then there would be a long silence, during which she completely ignored him.

At one point, she went out of the room through a door at the back, which she did not bother to shut behind her. The door presumably led into the kitchen. She was gone some time. They could hear her putting something on the stove. While she was

52

away, a little old man came in and, obviously knowing his way about, made straight for a corner table, and took a box of dominoes from the shelf underneath. He tipped the dominoes onto the table and jumbled them up, as though intending to play all by himself. The clink of the pieces brought the woman back from the kitchen. Without a word, she went to the bar and poured a pink apéritif, which she slapped down on the table in front of him.

The man waited. A few minutes later, another little old man came in and sat down opposite him. The two were so much alike that they could have been brothers.

"Am I late?"

"No. I was early."

Madame Calas poured an apéritif of a different sort, and carried it over to the table. On the way, she pressed a switch, and a light came on at the far end of the room. All without a word spoken, as in a mime.

"Doesn't she give you the creeps?" Lapointe whispered to Maigret. That was not the effect she had on the Superintendent. He was intensely interested in her, more so than in anyone he had met for a very long time.

Had he not in his youth dreamed of an ideal vocation for himself, a vocation which did not exist in real life? He had never told anyone, had never even given it a name, but he knew now what it was he had wanted to be: a guide to the lost.

In fact, curiously enough, in the course of his work as a policeman, he had often been able to help people back onto the right road, from which they had misguidedly strayed. More curiously still, recent years had seen the birth of a new vocation, similar in many respects to the vocation of his dreams: that of the psychoanalyst, whose function it is to bring a man face to face with his true self.

To be sure, he had discovered one of her secrets, though secret was perhaps hardly the word for something that all her regular customers must be aware of. Twice more she had retreated to the back room and, the second time, he had clearly heard the squeaking of a cork in a bottle.

She drank. He was quite sure of one thing. She never got drunk, never lost her self-control. Like all true alcoholics, whom doctors are powerless to help, she knew her own capacity. She drank only as much as was needed to maintain her in the state of anesthesia which had so puzzled him at their first meeting.

"How old are you?" he asked her, when she was back at her post behind the counter.

"Forty-one."

There was no hesitation. She said it without a trace of either coquetry or bitterness. She knew she looked older. No doubt she had stopped caring years ago about other people and what they thought of her. She looked worn out, with dark shadows under the eyes, a tremor at the corner of the mouth, and, already, slack folds under the chin. She must have lost a great deal of weight, judging by her dress, which was far too big, and hung straight down from her shoulders.

"Were you born in Paris?"

"No."

She must know, he felt sure, what lay behind his questions. Yet she did not shrink from them. She was giving nothing away, but at least he got a straight answer to a straight question.

The two old men, behind Maigret, were playing dominoes, as no doubt they did every evening at this time.

What puzzled Maigret was that she did her drinking out of sight. What was the point, seeing that she did not care what people thought of her, of slinking off into the back room to have her swig of wine or spirits, or whatever it was, straight out of the bottle? Could it be that she still retained this one vestige of self-respect? He doubted it. It is only when they are under supervision that hardened alcoholics resort to subterfuge.

Was that the answer? There was the husband, Omer Calas. He might well object to his wife's drinking, in front of the customers at least.

"Does your husband go regularly to Poitiers for his wine?"

"Every year."

"Once a year?"

"Sometimes twice. It depends."

"On what?"

"On our trade."

"Does he always go on a Friday?"

"I can't remember."

"Did he say he was going on a business trip?"

"To whom?"

"To you."

"He never tells me anything."

"Would he have mentioned it to any of the customers, or a friend?"

"I've no idea."

"Were those two here last Friday?"

"Not when Omer left. They never come in before five."

Maigret turned to Lapointe.

"Ring the Gare Montparnasse, will you, and find out the times of the afternoon trains to Poitiers. Have a word with the stationmaster."

Maigret spoke in an undertone. Had she been watching him, Madame Calas would have been able to lip-read the message, but she did not trouble to do so.

"Ask him to make inquiries among the station staff, especially in the ticket office. Have him get the husband's description."

The telephone booth, unlike most, was not at the far end of the room, but near the entrance. Lapointe asked for a *jeton*, and moved toward the glass door. Night was closing in, and there was a bluish mist outside. Maigret, who had his back to the door, heard quickening footsteps, and turned to catch a glimpse of a young face which, in the half-light, looked blurred and very pale. Then he saw the dark outline of a man running in the direction of La Villette, followed by Lapointe, who had wrenched open the door to dash out and give chase. He had not had time to shut the door behind him. Maigret went outside, and stood on the pavement. He could now barely see the two running figures, but even after they had disappeared from view he could still hear their rapid footsteps on the cobbles.

Lapointe must have seen a face he recognized through the glass door. Maigret had not seen very much, but he could guess what must have happened. The fugitive fitted the description of the errand boy who, earlier in the day, had watched the diver at work in the canal, and fled when approached by a policeman.

"Do you know him?" he asked Madame Calas.

"Who?"

It was no use pressing the point. Anyway, she might well have been looking the other way when it all happened.

"Is it always as quiet as this in here?"

"It depends."

"On what?"

"On the time of day. And some days are busier than others."

As though to prove it, a siren sounded, releasing the workers at a nearby factor, and a few minutes later there was a noise in the street like a column on the march. The door opened and shut and opened and shut again, a dozen times at least. People sat down at the tables, and others, like Maigret, stood at the bar.

Most of them seemed to be regulars, as the woman did not ask what they wanted, but silently poured their usual drinks.

"I see Omer's not home."

"No."

She did not go on to say: "He's out of town," or "He left for Poitiers on Friday."

She merely answered the question, and left it at that. What was her background? He could not even hazard a guess. Life had tarnished her, and eroded some part of her real self. Through drink, she had withdrawn into a private world of her own, and her links with reality were tenuous.

"Have you lived here long?"

"In Paris?"

"No. In this café."

"Twenty-four years."

"Was your husband here before you?"

"No."

He did some rapid mental arithmetic.

"So you were seventeen when you first met him?"

"I knew him before that."

"How old is he now?"

"Forty-seven."

This did not altogether tally with Doctor Paul's estimate of the man's age, but it was not far out. Not that Maigret was convinced he was on the right track. His questions were prompted more by personal curiosity than anything else. For it would surely be a miracle if, without the smallest effort on his part, he were to establish the identity of the headless corpse on the very first day of the inquiry.

There was a hum of voices in the bar, and a floating veil of tobacco smoke had formed overhead. People were coming and going. The two players, absorbed in their game of dominoes, seemed unaware that they were not the only people on earth.

"Do you have a photograph of your husband?"

"No."

"Not even a snapshot?"

"No."

"Have you got any of yourself?"

"No. Only the one on my identity card."

Not one person in a thousand, Maigret knew from experience, can claim not to possess a single personal photograph.

"Do you live upstairs?"

She nodded. He had seen from the outside that the building was a single-story structure. The space below street level comprised the café and kitchen. The floor above, he assumed, must consist of two or three rooms, more likely two, plus a lavatory or storeroom.

"How do you get up there?"

"The staircase is in the kitchen."

Shortly after this exchange, she went into the kitchen, and this time he heard her stirring something in a saucepan. The door burst open noisily, and Maigret saw Lapointe, flushed, bright-eyed and panting, pushing a young man ahead of him.

The little fellow, as Lapointe was always referred to at the Quai des Orfèvres, not because he was undersized but because he was the youngest and most junior of the Inspectors, had never looked so pleased with himself in his life.

"I didn't catch him until we were right at the end of the street!" he said, grinning broadly and reaching out for his glass, which was still on the counter. "Once or twice I thought he'd given me the slip. It's just as well I was the five-hundred-meter champion at school!"

The young man, too, was panting, and Maigret could feel his hot breath.

"I haven't done anything," he protested, appealing to Maigret.

"In that case, you have nothing to fear."

Maigret looked at Lapointe.

"Have you seen his identity card?"

"Just to be on the safe side, I kept it. It's in my pocket. He works as an errand boy for the Maison Pincemail. And he's the one who was snooping on the wharf this morning, and made a quick getaway when he saw he'd been noticed."

"What did you do that for?" Maigret asked the young man.

He scowled, as boys do when they want to show what tough guys they are.

"Well?"

"I've nothing to say."

"Didn't you get anything out of him on the way?" he asked Lapointe.

"We were both so winded we could hardly speak. His name is Antoine Cristin. He's eighteen, and he lives with his mother in rooms in the Faubourg Saint-Martin."

One or two people had turned around to look at them, but not with any great interest. In this district, a policeman bursting into a bar was quite a common sight.

"What were you up to out there?"

"Nothing."

"He had his nose pressed against the glass." Lapointe explained. "The minute I saw him. I remembered what Judel had said, and I nipped out to get him."

"If you had done nothing wrong, why try to get away?"

He hesitated, took a quick look around to satisfy himself that there were at least a couple of people within earshot, then said, with a theatrical curl of the lip: "Because I don't like cops."

"But you don't mind spying on them through glass doors?"

"There's no law against it."

"How did you know we were in here?"

"I didn't."

"What did you come for, then?"

He flushed, and bit his fleshy lower lip.

"Come on, let's have it."

"I was just passing."

"Do you know Omer?"

"I don't know anyone."

"Not even Madame?"

She was back in her place behind the bar, watching them. But there was no trace of fear or even anxiety in her face. Had she anything to hide? If so, her nerve was beyond anything Maigret had ever encountered in a criminal or accessory to a crime.

"Do you know her?"

"By sight."

"Don't you ever come in here for a drink?"

"Maybe."

"Where's your bicycle?"

"At the shop. I'm off at five."

Maigret made a sign to Lapointe, one of the few secret signs used by plain-clothes detectives. Lapointe nodded. He went into the telephone booth and rang, not the Gare Montparnasse, but the Police Station just across the road, and eventually he got hold of Judel.

"We've got the kid here, at Calas's place. In a minute or two, the boss will let him go, but he wants someone standing by in case he makes a run for it. Any news?"

"Nothing worth mentioning. Four or five reports of scuffles in bars on Sunday night; someone who thinks he heard a body being dropped in the water; a prostitute who claims she had her handbag snatched by an Arab . . ."

"So long."

Maigret, very bland, turned to the young man.

"What will you have, Antoine? Wine? Beer?"

"Nothing."

"Don't you drink?"

"Not with cops. I don't. You'll have to let me go, you know."

"You're very sure of yourself."

"I know my rights."

He was a broad-shouldered, sturdy country lad,

with a wholesome complexion. Paris had not yet robbed him of his robust health. Maigret could not count the number of times he had seen kids just like him end up having black-jacked some poor old soul in a tobacconist's or dry-goods shop, to rob the till of a couple of hundred francs.

"Have you any brothers or sisters?"

"I'm an only child."

"Where's your father?"

"He's dead."

"Does your mother go out to work?"

"She's a cleaning woman."

Maigret turned to Lapointe:

"Give him back his identity card. All in order, is it? The correct address, and so on?"

"Yes."

The boy looked uncertain, suspecting a trap.

"Can I go?"

"Whenever you like."

He went without a word of thanks or even a nod, but on his way out he winked furtively at the woman, a signal which did not escape Maigret.

"You'd better call the station now."

He ordered two more glasses of white wine. There were fewer people in the café now. Only three customers, other than Lapointe and himself, and the two old men playing dominoes.

"You don't know him, do you?"

"Who?"

"The young man who was here just now."

Unhesitatingly, she said:

"Yes."

It was as simple as that. Maigret was disconcerted.

"Does he come here often?"

62

"Quite often."

"For a drink?"

"He drinks very little."

"Beer?"

"And occasionally wine."

"Does he usually come in after work?"

"No."

"During the day?"

She nodded. Her unshakable composure was beginning to exasperate the Superintendent.

"When he happens to be passing."

"You mean when he's around this way on his bicycle? In other words, when he's out delivering?"

"Yes."

"And what time of day would that be?"

"Between half past three and four."

"Does he have a regular round?"

"I think so."

"Does he stand at the bar?"

"Sometimes he sits at a table."

"Which one?"

"This one over here, next to the till."

"Is he a particular friend of yours?"

"Yes."

"Why wouldn't he admit it?"

"He was showing off, I expect."

"Does he make a habit of it?"

"He does his best."

"Do you know his mother?"

"No."

"Are you from the same village?"

"No."

"He just walked in one day, and you made a friend of him. Is that it?"

"Yes."

"Half past three in the afternoon. That's when your husband is out playing billiards in a brasserie, isn't it?"

"Most days, yes."

"Is it just a coincidence, do you think, that Antoine should choose that particular time to visit you?"

"I've never thought about it."

Maigret hesitated before asking his next question. The very idea shocked him, but he had a feeling that there were even more shocking revelations to come.

"Does he make love to you?"

"It depends what you mean."

"Is he in love with you?"

"I dare say he likes me."

"Do you give him presents?"

"I slip him a note from the till, occasionally."

"Does your husband know?"

"No."

"Doesn't he notice that sort of thing?"

"He has, from time to time."

"Was he angry?"

"Yes."

"Isn't he suspicious of Antoine?"

"I don't think so."

Entering this dark room, two steps down from the street, they had stepped into another world, a world in which all the familiar values were distorted, in which even familiar words had a different meaning. Lapointe was still in the telephone booth, talking to the stationmaster.

"Will you forgive me, Madame Calas, if I ask you a more intimate question?"

"If you want to, you will, whatever I say."

"Is Antoine your lover?"

She did not flinch or even look away from Maigret.

"It has happened from time to time," she admitted.

"You mean to say you have had intercourse with him?"

"You'd have found out sooner or later, anyway. I'm sure he'll tell you himself before long."

"Has it happened often?"

"Quite often."

"Where?"

It was a question of some importance. Madame Calas, in the absence of her husband, had to be available to serve anyone who might happen to come in. Maigret glanced up at the ceiling. But could she be sure of hearing the door open, up there in the bedroom?

In the same straightforward manner in which she had answered all his questions, she nodded toward the open kitchen door at the back of the room.

"In there?"

"Yes."

"Were you ever interrupted?"

"Not by Omer."

"By whom?"

"One day, a customer wearing rubber-soled shoes came into the kitchen, because there was no one in the bar."

"What did he do?"

"He laughed."

"Didn't he tell Omer?"

"No."

"Did he ever come back?"

It was intuition that prompted Maigret to ask. So far he had judged Madame Calas correctly. Even his wildest shots had hit the target.

"Did he come back often?" he pressed her.

"Two or three times."

"While Antoine was here?"

"No."

It would not have been difficult to tell whether or not the young man was in the café. Any time earlier than five o'clock, he would have had to leave his delivery bicycle at the door.

"Were you alone?"

"Yes."

"And he made you go into the kitchen with him?"

For a second, there was a flicker of expression in her eyes. Mockery? Perhaps he had imagined it. All the same, he believed he could read an unspoken message there:

"Why ask, when you know the answer?"

She understood him as well as he understood her. They were a match for one another. To be more precise, life had taught them both the same lesson.

It all happened so quickly that Maigret wondered afterwards whether he had imagined the whole thing.

"Are there many others?" he asked, lowering his voice. His tone was almost confidential now.

"A few."

Then, standing very still, not bending forward toward her, he put one last question:

"Why?"

To that question, there was no answer but a

slight shrug. She was not one to strike romantic attitudes or dramatize her situation.

He had asked her why. If he did not know, it was not for her to tell him.

The fact was that he did know. He had only wanted confirmation. He had got it. There was no need for her to say anything.

He now knew to what depths she had sunk. What he still did not know was what had driven her there. Would she be equally ready to tell him the truth about her past?

That would have to wait. Lapointe had joined him at the bar. He gulped down some wine and then said:

"There's a weekday train to Poitiers that leaves at four forty-eight. The stationmaster says that neither of the ticket-office clerks remember anyone answering the descirption. He's going to make further inquiries, and call us at Headquarters. On the other hand, he thinks we'd do better to ring Poitiers. It's a slow train, and it goes on south from Poitiers, so there would have been fewer people stopping there than had boarded the train at Montparnasse."

"Put Lucas on to that. Tell him to ring Saint-Aubin and the nearest villages. Where there isn't a police station, let him try the local inn."

Lapointe asked Madame Calas for some *jetons*, and she handed them over listlessly. She asked no questions. Being interrogated about her husband's movements might have been an everyday occurrence. Yet she knew what had been found in the Saint-Martin Canal, and could not have been unaware of the search that had been going on all day almost under her windows.

"Did you see Antoine last Friday?"

"He never comes on Friday."

"Why not?"

"He has a different round that day."

"And after five o'clock?"

"My husband is usually back by then."

"So he wasn't here at any time during the afternoon or evening?"

"That's right."

"You've been married to Omer Calas for twenty-four years?"

"I've been living with him for twenty-four years."

"You're not married?"

"Yes. We were married at the Town Hall in the 10th *Arrondissement*, but not until sixteen or seventeen years ago. I can't remember exactly."

"No children?"

"One daughter."

"Does she live with you?"

"No."

"In Paris?"

"Yes."

"How old is she?"

"She's just twenty-four. I had her when I was seventeen."

"Is Omer the father?"

"Yes."

"No doubt about it?"

"None whatever."

"Is she married?"

"No."

"Does she live alone?"

"She's got rooms in the Ile Saint-Louis."

"Has she a job?"

"She's assistant to one of the surgeons at the Hôtel-Dieu, Professor Lavaud."

For the first time, she had told him more than was strictly necessary. Could it be that, in spite of everything, she still retained some vestige of natural feeling, and was proud of her daughter?

"Did you see her last Friday?"

"No."

"Does she ever come to see you?"

"Occasionally."

"When was the last time?"

"Three or four weeks ago."

"Was your husband here?"

"I think so."

"Does your daughter get on well with him?"

"She has as little to do with us as possible."

"Because she's ashamed of you?"

"Possibly."

"How old was she when she left home?"

There was a little color in her cheeks now, and a touch of defiance in her voice.

"Fifteen."

"Without warning?"

She nodded.

"Was there a man?"

She shrugged.

"I don't know. It makes no difference."

The room was empty now, except for the two old men. One was putting the dominoes back in their box, and the other was banging a coin on the table. Madame Calas got the message, and went over to refill their glasses.

"Isn't that Maigret?" one of them asked in an undertone.

"Yes."

69

"What does he want?"

"He didn't say."

Nor had she asked him. She went into the kitchen for a moment, came back to the bar, and said in a low voice:

"My meal is ready. Will you be long?"

"Where do you have your meals?"

"Over there." She pointed to a table at the far end of the room.

"I won't keep you much longer. Did your husband have an attack of appendicitis several years back?"

"Five or six years ago. He had an operation."

"Who did it?"

"Let me think. A Doctor Gran . . . Granvalet. That's it! He lived in the Boulevard Voltaire."

"Where is he now?"

"He died, or so we were told by another of his patients."

Had Granvalet been alive, he could have told them whether Omer Calas had a rainbow-shaped scar on his abdomen. Tomorrow, they would have to track down the assistants and nurses who had taken part in the operation. Unless, of course, they found Omer safe and well in some village inn near Poitiers.

"Was your husband ever, years ago, involved in a shotgun accident?"

"Not since I've known him."

"Did he ever join a shooting party?"

"He may have, when he lived in the country."

"Have you ever noticed a scar, rather faint, on his stomach, in the shape of a rainbow?"

She frowned, apparently trying to remember, and then shook her head.

"Are you sure?"

"I haven't seen him undressed for a very long time."

"Did you love him?"

"I don't know."

"How long did you remain faithful to him?"

"For years."

She said this with peculiar emphasis.

"Were you very young when you first knew each other?"

"We come from the same village."

"What village?"

"It's really a hamlet, about midway between Montargis and Gien. It's called Boissancourt."

"Do you go back there often?"

"Never."

"You've never been back?"

"No."

"Not since you and Omer came together?"

"I left when I was seventeen."

"Were you pregnant?"

"Six months."

"Was it generally known?"

"Yes."

"Did your parents know?"

In the same matter-of-fact tone, about which there was a kind ow nightmare quality, she said dryly:

"Yes."

"You never saw them again?"

"No."

Lapointe, having finished passing on Maigret's instructions to Lucas, came out of the telephone booth, mopping his brow.

"What do I owe you?" asked Maigret.

For the first time, she had a question to ask.
"Are you going?"
And, taking his tone from her, he replied,
"Yes."

Chapter 4

The Boy on the Roof

Maigret hesitated a long time before taking his pipe out of his pocket, which was most unlike him; and when he did, he assumed an absent-minded air, as though he had just got it out to keep his hands occupied while he was talking.

The staff meeting in the Chief's office had been short. When it was over, Maigret and the Chief stood for a few minutes talking by the open window, and then Maigret made straight for the little communicating door which led to the Department of Public Prosecutions. The benches all along the corridor in the Examining Magistrates' Wing were crowded, two police vans having driven into the courtyard a short while before. Maigret recognized most of the prisoners waiting handcuffed, between two guards, and one or two, apparently bearing him no ill-will, nodded a greeting as he went past.

By the time he had got back to his office the

previous evening, there were several messages on his pad requesting him to phone Judge Coméliau. The Judge was thin and nervy, with a little brown mustache that looked dyed, and the bearing of a cavalry officer. His very first words to Maigret were:

"I want to know exactly how things stand."

Obediently Maigret told him, beginning with Victor's search of the Saint-Martin Canal, and his failure to find the head. Even at this early stage, he was interrupted.

"The diver will be continuing the search today, I presume?"

"I didn't consider it necessary."

"It seems to me that, having discovered the rest of the body in the canal, it's logical to assume that the head can't be far away."

This was what made him so difficult to work with. He was not the only meddling magistrate, but he was certainly the most pig-headed. He wasn't a fool, by any means. It was said by lawyers who had known him in his student days that he had been one of the most brilliant men of his class.

One could only suppose that he had never learned to apply his intelligence to the hard facts of life. He was very much a man of the Establishment, guided by inflexible principles and hallowed taboos, which determined his attitude in all things. Patiently, the Chief Superintendent explained:

"In the first place, Judge, Victor is as much at home in the canal as you are in your office and I am in mine. He has gone over the bottom inch by inch, at least a couple of hundred times. He's a conscientious fellow. If he says the head isn't there . . ."

"My plumber is a conscientious fellow, too, and he knows his job, but that doesn't prevent him from assuring me, every time I send for him, that there can't possibly be any defect in my water system."

"It rarely happens, in the case of a dismembered corpse, that the head is found near the body."

Coméliau was making a visible effort, with his bright little eyes fixed on Maigret, who went on:

"It's understandable. It's no easy matter to identify a torso or a limb, especially when it's been some time in the water, but a head is easily recognizable. And because it's less cumbersome than a body, it's worth taking the trouble to dispose of it further afield."

"Yes, I'll grant you that."

Maigret, as discreetly as he could, had got out his tobacco pouch and was holding it in his left hand, hoping that something might distract the magistrate's attention, so that he could fill his pipe.

He turned to the subject of Madame Calas, and described the bar in the Quai de Valmy.

"What led you to her?"

"Pure chance, I must admit. I had a phone call to make, and there was no telephone booth in the first bar I went into, only a wall instrument, making private conversation impossible."

"Go on."

Maigret told him of Calas's alleged departure by train for Poitiers, and of the relationship between the proprietress of the bar and Antoine Cristin, the errand boy. And he did not forget to mention the crescent-shaped scar.

"Do you mean to tell me that you believed this

woman when she said she didn't know whether or not her husband had such a scar?"

This infuriated the Judge, because he could not understand it.

"To be perfectly frank, Maigret, I can't understand why you didn't have the woman and the boy brought in for questioning in the routine way. It's the usual practice, and generally produces results. I take it her story is a pack of lies?"

"Not necessarily."

"But claiming she didn't know where her husband was or when he would return . . . Well, really! . . ."

Coméliau was born in a house on the Left Bank, with a view over the Luxembourg. He was still living in it. How could such a man be expected to have the smallest insight into the minds of people like Omer Calas and his wife?

At last! The flicker of a match, and Maigret's pipe was alight. Now for the disapproving stare. Coméliau had a perfect horror of smoking, and this was his way of showing it when anyone had the impudence to light up in his presence. Maigret, however, was determined to outface him.

"You may be right," he conceded. "She could have been lying to me. On the other hand, she could have been telling the truth. All we have is a dismembered corpse without a head. All we know for certain is that the dead man was aged between forty-five and fifty-five. So far, he has not been identified. Do you imagine that Calas is the only man to have disappeared in the past few days, or gone off without saying where? Madame Calas is a secret drinker, and her lover, the errand boy, is scared of the police. Does that give me the right to have her brought to Headquarters as a suspect? What kind of fools will we look if, in the next day or so, a head is found, and it turns out not to be the head of Omer Calas at all?"

"Are you having the house watched?"

"Judel of the 10th *Arrondissement* has a man posted on the quay, and I went back myself after dinner last night to take a look around."

"Did you get any results?"

"Nothing much. I stopped one or two prostitutes in the street, and asked them a few questions. It's one of those districts where the atmosphere is quite different at night from what it is by day, and I was hoping that if there was anything suspicious going on around the café on Sunday night, one of these women would have seen or heard it."

"Did you discover anything?"

"Not much. I did get what may be a lead from one of them, but I haven't had time to follow it up.

"According to her, the woman Calas has another lover, a middle-aged man with red hair, who either lives or works in the district. My informant, it must be admitted, is eaten up with spite, because, as she put it, 'that woman takes the bread out of our mouths.' If she were a pro, she said, they wouldn't mind so much. But she does it for nothing. All the men, it seems, know where to go. They only have to wait till the husband's back is turned. No one is refused, I'm told, though, of course, I haven't put it to the test."

In the face of such depravity, Coméliau could only heave a distressful sigh.

"You must proceed as you think fit, Maigret. I don't see any problem myself. There's no need to handle people of that sort with kid gloves."

"I shall be seeing her again shortly. And I intend to see the daughter as well. As to identification, I hope we shall be able to clear that up through the nurses who were present at the operation on Calas five years ago."

In that connection, one curious fact had emerged. The previous evening, while Maigret was wandering about the streets, he had suddenly remembered another question he wanted to put to Madame Calas, and had gone back to the bistro. Madame Calas was sitting half asleep on a chair and four men were playing cards at a table. Maigret had asked her the name of the hospital where her husband had been operated on.

He had formed an impression of Calas as a fairly tough character, not at all the sort to pamper himself, fret about his health, or fear for his life. Yet when it came to undergoing a simple operation, without complications, virtually without risk, he had not chosen to go into hospital but, at considerable expense, to a private clinic at Villejuif. And not just any private clinic, but a religious establishment, staffed by nuns.

Maigret looked at his watch. Lapointe must be there by now. He would soon be telephoning to report.

"Be firm, Maigret!" urged Coméliau, as the Superintendent was leaving.

It was not lack of firmness that was holding him back. It was not pity either. Coméliau would never understand. The world into which Maigret had suddenly been plunged was so different from the familiar world of daily life that he could only feel his way, tentatively, step by step. Was there any connection between the occupants of the little café in the Quai de Valmy and the corpse thrown into the Saint-Martin Canal? Possibly. But it was equally possible that it was mere coincidence.

He returned to his office, feeling restless and disgruntled, as he nearly always did at this stage of any inquiry.

Last night, he had been collecting and storing information without stopping to consider where it was all leading. Now, he was faced with a jumble of facts which needed sorting out and piecing together.

Madame Calas was no longer simply a colorful character, such as he occasionally encountered in his work. She was his problem, his responsibility.

Coméliau saw her as a sexually promiscuous, drink-sodden degenerate. That was not how Maigret saw her. Just what she was, he could not say yet, and until he knew for sure, until he felt the truth in his bones, as it were, he would be oppressed by this indefinable uneasiness.

Lucas was in his office. He had just put the mail on his desk.

"Any new developments?"

"Have you been in the building all the time, sir?"

"With Coméliau."

"If I'd known, I'd have had your calls transferred. Yes, there has been a new development. Judel is in a terrible stew."

It was Madame Calas who came at once into Maigret's mind, and he wondered what could have happened to her. But it had nothing to do with her.

"It's about the young man, Antoine. I think that was the name."

79

"Yes, Antoine. What's happened? Has he vanished again?"

"That's it. It seems you left instructions last night that he was to be kept under observation. The young man went straight to his lodgings, at the far end of the Faubourg Saint-Martin, almost at the junction with the Rue Louis-Blanc. The man detailed to follow him had a word with the concierge. The boy lives with his mother, who is a cleaning woman, on the seventh floor of the building. They have two attic rooms. There's no elevator. I got all this from Judel, of course. Apparently, the building is one of those ghastly great tenements, housing fifty or sixty families, with swarms of kids spilling out onto the stairs."

"Go on."

"That's about all. According to the concierge, the boy's mother is an estimable woman with plenty of guts. Her husband died in a sanatorium. She has had TB herself. She claims to be cured, but the concierge doubts it. Well, when he had heard all this, Judel's man rang the Station for further instructions. Judel, not wanting to take any chances, told him to stay where he was and watch the building. He stood guard outside until about midnight. All the tenants were in by then. He went in after the last of them, and spent the night on the stairs.

"This morning, just before eight, a thin woman went past the lodge, and the concierge called out to him that this was Antoine's mother. He saw no necessity to stop or follow her. It was not until half an hour later that, having nothing better to do, he thought of going up to the seventh floor, to have a look around.

"It did strike him as odd then that the boy hadn't

yet left for work. He listened at the keyhole, but couldn't hear a sound. He knocked, and got no answer. In the end, after examining the lock and seeing that it was anything but secure, he decided to use his skeleton keys.

"The first room he came to was the kitchen. There was a bed in it, the mother's bed. In the other room there was a bed too, unmade. But there was no one there, and the skylight was open.

"Judel is furious with himself for not having foreseen this, and given instructions accordingly. It's obvious that the kid got out through the skylight during the night, and crawled along the rooftops looking for another open skylight. He probably got out through a building in the Rue Louis-Blanc."

"They've checked that he's not hiding in the tenement, I take it?"

"They're still questioning the tenants."

Maigret could imagine Judge Coméliau's sarcastic smile when he was told about this.

"Nothing from Lapointe?"

"Not yet."

"Has anyone turned up at the mortuary to identify the corpse?"

"Only the regulars."

There were about a dozen of these, elderly women for the most part, who, every time a body was found, rushed to the mortuary to identify it.

"Didn't Doctor Paul ring?"

"I've just put his report on your desk."

"If you speak to Lapointe, tell him to come back here and wait for me. I won't be far away."

He walked toward the Ile Saint-Louis. He skirted Notre-Dame, crossed a little iron footbridge, and soon found himself in the narrow, crowded Rue Saint-Louis-en-l'Ile. The housewives were all out doing their shopping at this time of day, and he had difficulty in pushing past them as they crowded around the little market stalls. Maigret found the grocer's shop above which, according to Madame Calas, her daughter Lucette had a room. He went down the little alleyway at the side of the shop and came to a cobbled courtyard shaded by a lime tree, like the forecourt of a village school or country vicarage.

"Looking for someone?" shrilled a woman's voice from a window on the ground floor.

"Mademoiselle Calas."

"Third floor, left-hand side, but she's not at home."

"Do you know when she'll be back?"

"She very seldom comes home for lunch. She's not usually back before half past six in the evening. If it's urgent, you can get her at the hospital."

The Hôtel-Dieu, where Lucette Calas worked, was not far away. All the same, it was no easy matter to find Professor Lavaud. This was the busiest time of the day. The corridors were crowded with hurrying men and women in white coats, nurses pushing trolleys, patients taking their first uncertain steps. There were doors opening on-to other corridors leading heaven knows where.

"Please can you tell me where I can find Mademoiselle Calas?"

They hardly noticed him.

"Don't know. Is she a patient?"

Or they pointed to a corridor.

"Down there."

He was told to go first in one direction and then

in another, until at last he reached a corridor where stillness and silence reigned. It was like coming into port after a voyage. Except for a girl seated at a table, it was deserted.

"Mademoiselle Calas?"

"Is it personal business? How did you manage to get this far?"

He must have penetrated one of those sanctums not accessible to ordinary mortals. He gave his name, and even went so far as to produce his credentials, so little did he feel he had any standing here.

"I'll go and see if she can spare you a minute or two, but I'm afraid she may be in the operating theater."

He was kept waiting a good ten minutes, and he dared not light his pipe. When the girl came back she was accompanied by a nurse, rather tall, with an air of self-possession and serenity.

"Are you the gentleman who wished to see me?"

"Chief Superintendent Maigret from Police Headquarters."

The contrast with the bar in the Quai de Valmy seemed all the greater on account of the cleanliness and brightness of the hospital, the white uniform and starched cap of the nurse.

Lucette Calas seemed more astonished than distressed. Obviously, she had not the least idea what he had come about.

"Are you sure I'm the person you want to see?"

"You are the daughter of Monsieur and Madame Calas, of the Quai de Valmy, aren't you?"

It was gone in a flash, but Maigret was sure he had seen a spark of resentment in her eyes.

"Yes, but I . . ."

"There are just one or two questions I'd like to ask you."

"I can't spare much time. The Professor will be starting his round of the wards shortly, and . . ."

"It will only take a few minutes."

She shrugged, looked around, and pointed to an open door.

"We'd better go in there."

There were two chairs, an adjustable couch for examining patients, and a few surgical instruments that Maigret could not identify.

"Is it long since you last saw your parents?"

She started at the word "parents," and Maigret thought he knew why.

"I see as little of them as possible."

"Why is that?"

"Have you seen them?"

"I've seen your mother."

She was silent. What more explanation was needed?

"Have you anything against them?"

"What should I have, except that they brought me into the world?"

"You weren't there last Sunday?"

"I was out of town. It was my day off. I spent it in the country with friends."

"So you can't say where your father is?"

"You really should tell me what this is all about. You turn up here and start asking questions about two people who admittedly are, in the strictly legal sense, my parents, but from whom I have been totally estranged for years. Why? Has something happened to him?"

She lit a cigarette, saying:

"Smoking is allowed in here. At this time of day, at any rate."

But he did not take advantage of this opportunity to light his pipe.

"Would it surprise you to hear that something had happened to one or the other of them?"

She looked him straight in the eye, and said flatly:

"No."

"What would you expect to hear?"

"That Calas's brutality to my mother had gone too far for once."

She did not refer to him as "my father," but as "Calas."

"Does he often resort to physical violence?"

"I don't know about now. It used to be an almost daily occurrence."

"Didn't your mother object?"

"She put up with it. She may even have liked it."

"Have you any other possibilities in mind?"

"Maybe she put poison in his soup."

"Why? Does she hate him?"

"All I know is that she's lived with him for twenty-four years, and has never made any attempt to get away from him."

"Is she unhappy, do you think?"

"Look, Superintendent, I do my best not to think about her at all. As a child I had only one ambition—escape. And as soon as I could stand on my own feet, I got out."

"I know. You were just fifteen."

"Who told you?"

"Your mother."

"Then he hasn't killed her."

She looked thoughtful, then, raising her eyes to his, said:

"Is it him?"

"What do you mean?"

"Has she poisoned him?"

"I shouldn't think so. We don't even know for sure whether anything has happened to him. Your mother says he left for Poitiers on Friday afternoon. He goes there regularly, it seems, to get his supplies of white wine from the vineyards around there."

"That's right. He did even when I lived with them."

"A body has been recovered from the Saint-Martin Canal. It may be his."

"Has no one identified it?"

"Not so far. The difficulty is that the head has not been found."

Was it perhaps because she worked in a hospital that she did not even blench?

"How do you think it happened?" she asked.

"I don't know. I'm feeling my way. There seems to be several men in your mother's life, if you'll forgive my mentioning it."

"You surely don't imagine it's news to me!"

"Do you know whether your father, in childhood or adolescence, was wounded in the stomach by a shotgun?"

She looked surprised.

"I never heard him mention it."

"You never saw the scars, of course?"

"Well, if it was a stomach wound . . ." she protested, with the beginning of a smile.

"When were you last at the Quai de Valmy?"

"Let me think. It must be a month or more."

"Was it just a casual visit, keeping in touch with home, as it were?"

"Not exactly."

"Was Calas there?"

"I make it my business only to go there when he's out."

"In the afternoon, was it?"

"Yes, he's always out then, playing billiards somewhere near the Gare de l'Est."

"Was there a man with your mother?"

"Not on that occasion."

"Did you have any special reason for going to see her?"

"No."

"What did you talk about?"

"I can't remember. One thing and another."

"Was Calas mentioned?"

"I doubt it."

"You wouldn't by any chance have gone to ask your mother for money?"

"You're on the wrong track there, Superintendent. Rightly or wrongly, I have too much pride for that. There have been times when I've gone short of money, and, for that matter, food, but I've never gone to them begging for help. All the more reason not to do so now, when I'm earning a good living."

"Can't you recall anything that was said on that last occasion at the Quai de Valmy?"

"Nothing special."

"Among the men you saw in the bar from time to time, do you remember a fresh-complexioned youth who rides a delivery bicycle?"

She shook her head.

"Or a middle-aged man with red hair?"

This did strike a chord.

"With smallpox scars?" she asked.

"I don't know."

"If so, it's Monsieur Dieudonné."

"Who is Monsieur Dieudonné?"

"I know very little about him. A friend of my mother's. He's been going to the café for years."

"In the afternoon?"

She knew what he meant.

"Whenever I've seen him, it's been in the afternoon. But you may be wrong about him. I can't say for sure. He struck me as a quiet sort of man, the kind one thinks of as sitting by the fire after dinner in his slippers. Come to think of it, he always seems to be sitting by the stove, facing my mother. They behave like people who have known each other for a very long time. They take one another for granted, if you see what I mean. They could be mistaken for an old married couple."

"Do you happen to know his address?"

"He's got a muffled kind of voice. I'd know it again if I heard it. I've known him get up and say: 'Time to get back to work.' I imagine his place of work must be somewhere near there, but I don't even know what he does. He doesn't dress like a manual worker. He might be a bookkeeper, or something of the sort."

A bell sounded in the corridor. The girl sprang to her feet.

"It's for me," she said. "I'll have to go, I'm afraid."

"I may have to take up a little more of your time. If so, I'll call on you in the Rue Saint-Louis-en-l'Ile."

"I'm never there except in the evening. Please don't make it too late. I go to bed early."

He watched her go down the corridor. She was shaking her head slightly, puzzled by what she had just heard.

"Excuse me, Mademoiselle. How do I get out of here?"

He looked so lost that the girl at the desk smiled, got up, and led him along the corridor to a staircase.

"You'll manage all right from here. Down the stairs, then left, and left again."

"Thank you."

He did not have the temerity to ask her what she thought of Lucette Calas. He scarcely knew what he thought of her himself.

He stopped at a bar opposite the Palais de Justice for a glass of white wine. When, a few minutes later, he got back to his office, he found Lapointe waiting for him.

"Well, how did you make out with the nuns?"

"They couldn't have been nicer. I expected it to be rather an embarrassing experience, but they made me feel quite at home . . ."

"What about the scars?"

Lapointe was less enthusiastic on this subject.

"In the first place, the doctor who did the operation died three years ago, as Madame Calas told us. The sister in charge of records showed me the file. There's no mention of any scar, which isn't surprising. On the other hand, I did discover one thing: Calas had a stomach ulcer."

"Did they operate?"

"No. Apparently they always do extensive tests before an operation, and record their findings."

"There's no reference to any distinguishing marks."

"None at all. The sister very kindly went and spoke to the nuns who were present at the operation. None of them remembered Calas very clearly. One thought she remembered his asking for time to say his prayers before they gave him the anesthetic."

"Was he a Catholic?"

"No, he was scared. That's the kind of thing nuns don't forget. They wouldn't have noticed the scars."

They were back where they started, with a headless corpse that could not be identified with any certainty.

"What do we do next?" murmured Lapointe.

With Maigret in his present disgruntled mood, he judged it wiser to keep his voice down.

Perhaps Judge Coméliau was right after all. If the man found in the Saint-Martin Canal was Omer Calas, then it might indeed be true that there was no way of getting the evidence they needed except by subjecting his wife to cross-examination. A heart-to-heart talk with Antoine, the fellow with the bicycle, if only they could lay their hands on him, would also be helpful.

"Come on."

"Shall I get the car?"

"Yes."

"Where are we going?"

"To the canal."

On his way out, he gave instructions to the Inspectors concerned to order a search in the 10th *Arrondissement* for a red-haired man with a pock-marked face, Christian name: Dieudonné.

The car nosed its way between buses and trucks.

When they came to the Boulevard Richard-Lenoir, and were almost at Maigret's own front door, he suddenly growled:

"Take me to the Gare de l'Est."

Lapointe looked at him in bewilderment.

"There may be nothing to it, but I'd like to check all the same. We were told that Calas had a suitcase with him, when he left on Friday afternoon. Suppose he came back on Saturday. If he's the man, then whoever killed and dismembered him must have got rid of the suitcase somehow. I'm quite sure it isn't still in the house at the Quai de Valmy, and I bet you we won't find the clothes he's supposed to have been wearing there, either."

Lapointe nodded agreement.

"No suitcase has been recovered from the canal, nor any clothes, in spite of the fact that the dead man was stripped before being carved up."

"And the head hasn't been found!" exclaimed Lapointe, taking it a stage further.

There was nothing original about Maigret's reasoning. It was just a matter of experience. Six murderers out of ten, if they have anything incriminating to get rid of, deposit it in the luggage checkroom of a railway station.

And it was no distance from the Quai de Valmy to the Gare de l'Est.

Lapointe eventually found somewhere to park the car, and he followed Maigret to the luggage checkroom.

"Were you on duty last Sunday afternoon?" he asked the clerk.

"Only up to six o'clock."

"Did you take in a lot of luggage?"

"Not more than usual."

"Have any suitcases deposited on Sunday not been claimed yet?"

The clerk walked along the shelves, where suitcases and parcels of all shapes and sizes were stacked.

"Two," he said.

"Both left by the same person?"

"No. The ticket numbers aren't consecutive. The canvas carryall, anyway, was left by a woman, a fat woman. I remember her because of the smell of cheese."

"Are there cheeses in it?"

"No, the smell has gone. Maybe it was the woman herself."

"What about the other one?"

"It's a brown suitcase."

He pointed to a cheap, battered case.

"Is it labeled?"

"No."

"Can you describe the person who handed it in?"

"I could be wrong, but I'd swear it was a country fellow."

"Why a country fellow?"

"That's how he struck me."

"Because of his complexion?"

"Could be."

"What was he wearing?"

"A leather jacket, if I remember rightly, and a peaked cap."

Maigret and Lapointe exchanged glances. Antoine Christin was in both their minds.

"What time would it have been?"

"Round about five. Yes. A little after five, because the express from Strasbourg had just come in."

"If anyone comes to claim the case, will you please ring the Police Station at the Quai de Jemmapes immediately."

"What if the fellow takes fright and runs?"

"We'll be here, anyway, within minutes."

There was only one way of getting the suitcase identified. Madame Calas would have to be brought to see it.

She looked up mechanically when the two men came in, and went to the bar to serve them.

"We won't have anything just now," said Maigret. "Something has been found which you may be able to identify. The Inspector will take you to see it. It's not far from here."

"Had I better close the bar?"

"There's no need. It will only take a few minutes. I'll stay here."

She did not put on a hat. She merely changed out of her slippers into shoes.

"Will you tend to the customers?"

"I doubt if it will be necessary."

Maigret lingered for a moment on the pavement, watching Lapointe drive off with Madam Calas beside him. His face broke into a mischievous smile. He had never before been left all by himself in a bistro, just as if he owned it. He was so tickled by the notion that he went inside and slipped behind the bar.

Chapter 5

The Bottle of
Ink

The patches of sunlight were exactly where they
had been the morning before. One, on the rounded
end of the zinc counter, was shaped like an animal,
another fell like a spotlight on a print of a woman
in a red dress, holding a glass of foaming beer.

The little café, as Maigret had felt the previous
day, like so many of the cafés and bars in Paris,
had something of the atmosphere of a country inn,
deserted most of the week, suddenly coming to life
on market day.

Although he was tempted to help himself to a
drink, he could not permit himself to give way to
such a childish whim. Sternly, with his hands in his
pockets and his pipe clenched between his teeth,
he went over to the door at the back.

He had not yet seen what lay behind that door,
through which Madame Calas was always dis-
appearing. Not surprisingly, he found a kitchen,

94

rather untidy, but less dirty than he would have expected. Immediately to the left of the door was a dresser, painted brown, on which stood an open bottle of brandy. So, wine was not her tipple, but brandy, which—since there was no glass to be seen —she presumably swigged straight out of the bottle.

A window looked onto the courtyard, and there was a glass door, which was not locked. He pushed it open. Stacked in a corner were barrels, discarded straw wrappers, and broken buckets. There were rust-rings everywhere. Paris seemed far away, so much so that it would not have surprised him to find a mass of bird droppings, and hens scratching about.

Beyond the courtyard was a cul-de-sac, bounded on both sides by a blank wall, and presumably leading off a side road.

Mechanically, he looked up at the first-floor windows of the bistro. They were very dirty, and hung with faded curtains. Was there a flicker of movement up there, or had he imagined it? It was not the cat, which he had left stretched out by the stove.

He went back into the kitchen, taking his time, and then up the spiral staircase which led to the floor above. The treads creaked. There was a faint musty smell, which reminded him of little village inns at which he had stayed.

There were two doors on the landing. He opened the first, and was in what must have been the Calases' bedroom. The windows looked out onto the Quai de Valmy. The double bed, of walnut, had not been made that morning, but the sheets were reasonably clean. The furniture was what one would expect in this sort of household, old, heavy stuff, handed down from father to son, and glowing with the patina of age.

A man's clothes were hanging in the wardrobe. Between the windows stood an armchair covered with red plush and, beside it, an old-fashioned radio set. The only other furniture was a round table in the middle of the room, covered with a cloth of indeterminate color, and a couple of mahogany chairs.

No sooner had he come into the room than he felt that something was not quite as it should be. What was it? He looked searchingly about him. Once again, his glance rested on the table covered with a cloth. On it was a bottle of ink, apparently unopened, a cheap pen, and one of those blotters advertising an apéritif that are often put on café tables for the convenience of customers. He opened the blotter, not expecting to find anything of interest, and indeed he found nothing but three blank sheets of paper. Just then, he thought he heard a board creak. He listened. That sound had not come from the lavatory, which led off the bedroom. Returning to the landing, he opened the door to the other room, which was as large as the first. It was used as a storeroom, and was piled high with battered and broken furniture, old magazines, glasses and other bric-à-brac.

"Is there anyone there?" he called loudly, almost certain that he was not alone in the room.

For a moment, he stood absolutely still, and then, without making a sound, shot out his arm and jerked open a cupboard.

"No tricks this time!" he said.

It did not greatly surprise him to discover that it was Antoine cowering there in the cupboard, like a trapped animal.

"I thought it wouldn't be long before I found you. Come on out of there!"

"Are you arresting me?"

The young man, terrified, was staring at the handcuffs which the Superintendent had taken out of his pocket.

"I haven't made up my mind yet what I'm going to do with you, but I'm not having any more of your Indian rope tricks. Hold out your hands."

"You've got no right. I haven't done anything."

"Hold out your hands!"

He could see that the boy was only waiting for a chance to make a dash for it. He moved toward him and, leaning forward with all his weight, pinned him against the wall. When the boy had tired of kicking him in the shins, Maigret managed to fasten on the handcuffs.

"Now then, come along with me!"

"What has my mother been saying?"

"I don't know what she's going to say about all this, but, as far as we're concerned, we want to know the answers to a few questions."

"I'm saying nothing."

"You come along with me, just the same."

He motioned him forward. They went through the kitchen and into the bar. Antoine looked around, startled by the emptiness and the silence.

"Where is she?"

"The proprietress? Don't worry, she'll be back."

"Have you arrested her?"

"Sit down over there, and don't move!"

"I'm not taking orders from you!"

He had seen so many of them at that age, all more or less in the same plight, that he had come to expect the defiant posturing and back talk.

It would please Judge Coméliau, at any rate, that Antoine had been caught, though he himself did not believe that they would learn much from him.

The street door was pushed open, and a middle-aged man came in. He looked around in surprise, seeing Maigret very much in command in the middle of the room, and no Madame Calas.

"Is Madame not here?"

"She won't be long."

Had the man seen the handcuffs and, realizing that Maigret was a police officer, decided that discretion was the better part of valor? At any rate, he touched his cap, muttered something like "I'll come back later," and beat a hasty retreat.

He could not have got as far as the end of the street when the black car drew up at the door. Lapointe got out first, opened the door for Madame Calas, and then took a brown suitcase from the trunk.

She saw Antoine at first glance, frowned, and looked anxiously at Maigret.

"Didn't you know he was hiding upstairs?"

"Don't answer!" urged the young man. "He has no right to arrest me—I've done nothing. I challenge him to prove anything against me."

Briskly, Maigret turned to Lapointe.

"Is the suitcase his?"

"She didn't seem too sure at first, then she said it was, then that she couldn't swear to it without seeing what was in it."

"Did you open it?"

"I wanted you to be present. I signed for it, but the clerk was most insistent that he must have an official requisition as soon as possible."

"Get Coméliau to sign it. Is the clerk still there?"

"I imagine so. I couldn't persuade him to leave his post."

"Call him. Ask him to try and get someone to take over from him for a quarter of an hour. That shouldn't be too difficult. Tell him to hop into a taxi and come here."

"I understand," said Lapointe, looking at Antoine. Would the baggage clerk recognize him? If so, it would make everything a lot easier.

"Phone Moers as well. I want him here too, with a search warrant. And tell him to bring the photographers."

"Right you are, sir."

Madame Calas, who was standing in the middle of the room as though she were a stranger to the place, asked, as Antoine had done before her:

"Are you going to arrest me?"

"Why should I?" countered Maigret. She looked at him in bewilderment.

"Am I free to come and go?"

"In the house, yes."

He knew what she wanted, and, sure enough, she went into the kitchen and disappeared, making straight for the bandy bottle, no doubt. To lend color to her presence there, she rattled the crockery, and changed out of her shoes—which must have been pinching her, since she so seldom wore them—into slippers.

When she returned to her place behind the counter, she was herself again.

"Can I get you anything?"

"Yes, a glass of white wine—and one for the Inspector. Perhaps Antoine would like a beer?"

His manner was unhurried, hesitant even, as though he had not quite made up his mind what to do next. He took a leisurely sip of wine, and then went over to the door and locked it.

"Have you the key of the suitcase?"

"No."

"Do you know where it is?"

In "his" pocket, she supposed.

In Calas's pocket, since, according to her, he had his suitcase with him when he left the house.

"Have you a pair of pliers or a wrench of some sort?"

She took her time getting the pliers. Maigret lifted the suitcase onto a table. He waited for Lapointe to come out of the phone booth before forcing the flimsy lock.

"I've ordered a white wine for you."

"Thank you, sir."

The metal buckled and eventually broke. Maigret lifted the lid. Madame Calas had not moved from behind the counter. She was watching them, but did not seem greatly concerned.

In the suitcase were a gray suit of quite good quality, a pair of shoes, almost new, shirts, socks, razor, comb, toothbrush, and a cake of soap still in its wrapping.

"Are these your husband's things?"

"I suppose so."

"Aren't you sure?"

"He has a suit like that."

"And it's not in the wardrobe?"

"I haven't looked."

She was no help, but, at the same time, she did not hinder them. As before, her answers to questions were curt and guarded, though, unlike Antoine, she was not on the defensive.

While Antoine was scared stiff, the woman gave

the impression of having nothing to fear. The comings and goings of the police seemed to be a matter of indifference to her. They could carry on, as far as she was concerned, whatever they might discover.

"Anything strike you as odd?" Maigret said to Lapointe, while they were rummaging in the suitcase.

"You mean everything shoved in higgledy-piggledy like that?"

"Well, that's how most men would pack a suitcase. But there's something else. Calas, or so we're told, was setting out on a journey. He took a spare suit, and a change of shoes and underclothes. It's reasonable to assume that he packed the case upstairs in his bedroom."

Two men in housepainters' overalls rattled at the door, peered in through the glass, mouthed inaudible words, and went away.

"If that is so, can you think of any reason why he should have taken his dirty washing with him?"

One of the two shirts had, in fact, been worn, as well as a pair of trousers and a pair of socks.

"Do you mean you think someone else may have put the stuff in the suitcase?"

"He could have done it himself. The likelihood is that he did. But not at the start of his journey. He was packing to come home."

"I see what you mean."

"Did you hear what I said, Madame Calas?"

She nodded.

"Do you still maintain that your husband left on Friday afternoon, taking the suitcase with him?"

"I can only repeat what I have already told you."

"You're sure you don't mean Thursday, Friday being when he came back?"

She shook her head.

"Whatever I say, you'll believe what you want to believe."

A taxi drew up at the door. Maigret went to open it. As the station clerk got out, he said:

"It can wait. I won't keep you a minute."

The Superintendent ushered him into the café. The man looked about him, taking his time over it, getting his bearings, wondering what it was all about.

His glance rested on Antoine, who was still sitting on a bench in the corner. Then he turned to Maigret, opened his mouth, and gave Antoine another searching look.

All this time, which seemed longer than it was, Antoine was scowling defiance at him.

"I really do believe," began the man, scratching his head. He was conscientious, and there was some doubt in his mind.

"Well then! From what I can see of him, I'd say he was the one."

"You're lying," shouted the young man furiously.

"Maybe I ought to see what he looks like standing up."

"Stand up."

"No."

"Stand up!"

Maigret heard Madame Calas's voice behind him.

"Get up, Antoine."

The clerk looked at him thoughtfully.

"I'm almost sure," he murmured. "Does he wear a leather jacket?"

"Go and have a look upstairs in the back room," said Maigret to Lapointe.

They waited in silence. The station employee glanced toward the bar. Maigret could take a hint.

"A glass of white wine?" he asked.

"I wouldn't say no."

Lapointe returned with the jacket that Antoine had worn the previous day.

"Put it on."

The young man looked to the woman for guidance, resigned himself grudgingly, and held out his wrists for the handcuffs to be removed.

"Can't you see, he's just trying to suck up to the cops? They're all the same. Mention the word 'police,' and they shake in their shoes. Well, what about it? Do you still say you've seen me before?"

"I think so, yes."

"You're lying."

The clerk addressed himself to Maigret. He spoke calmly, though it was possible to detect an undercurrent of feeling in his voice.

"This is a serious business, I imagine. I shouldn't like to get an innocent person into trouble. This boy looks like the one who deposited the suitcase at the station on Sunday. Naturally, not knowing that anyone was going to ask me about him, I didn't take much notice of him. Perhaps if I saw him in the same place, under the same conditions, lighting and so on . . ."

"I'll have him brought to you at the station sometime today or tomorrow," said Maigret. "Thank you. Your very good health!"

He saw him to the door, and locked it after him. There was, in the Chief Superintendent's attitude to the case, a kind of diffidence that puzzled La-

pointe. He could not have said when he had begun
to notice it. Perhaps the previous day, right at the
start of the inquiry, when they had come together
to the Quai de Valmy, and pushed open the door
of the Calas bistro.

Maigret was pursuing his investigations in the
normal way, doing all that was required of him, but
surely with a lack of conviction that was the last
thing any of his subordinates would have expected
of him? It was difficult to define. Half-heartedness?
Reluctance? Disinclination? The facts of the case
interested him very little. He seemed to be wrapped
up in his thoughts, which he was keeping very much
to himself.

It was particularly noticeable here in the café,
especially when he was talking to Madame Calas,
or furtively watching her.

It was as though the victim were of no account,
and the dismembered corpse meant nothing to him.
He had virtually ignored Antoine, and it was only
with an effort that he was able to attend to the
routine aspects of his work.

"Phone Coméliau. I'd rather you did it. Just give
him a summary of events. You'd better ask him to
sign a warrant for the arrest of the kid. He'll do
it in any case."

"What about her?" asked the Inspector, pointing
to the woman.

"I'd rather not."

"What if he insists?"

"He'll have to have his own way. He's the boss."

He had not bothered to lower his voice, in spite
of the presence of the other two, whom he knew
to be listening.

"You'd better have a bite to eat." he advised

Madame Calas. "It may not be long before you have to go."

"For long?"

"For as long as the Judge thinks fit to hold you for questioning."

"Will they keep me in prison?"

"At the Central Police Station to begin with, I expect."

"What about me?" Antoine asked.

"You too. But not in the same cell!" Maigret added.

"Are you hungry?" Madame Calas asked the boy.

"No."

She went into the kitchen just the same, but it was to have a swig of brandy. When she came back, she asked:

"Who will look after the place when I'm gone?"

"No one. Don't worry. It will be kept under supervision."

He was still watching her with that same thoughtful expression. He could not help himself. It seemed to him that he had never encountered anyone so baffling.

He had experience of artful women, some of whom had stood up to him for a long time. In every case, however, he had felt from the first that he would have the last word. It was just a matter of time, patience, and determination.

With Madame Calas, it was different. She did not fit into any category. If he were to be told that she had murdered her husband in cold blood, and had carved him up single-handed on the kitchen table, he would not have found it impossible to believe. But he would not have found it impossible to believe, either, that she simply did not know what had become of her husband.

There she was in front of him, a living creature of flesh and blood, thin and faded in her dark dress, which hung from her shoulders like a shabby window-curtain. She was real enough, with the fire of her inner life smoldering in her somber eyes, and yet there was about her something insubstantial, elusive.

Was she aware of the impression she created? One would say so, judging from the cool, perhaps even ironic manner in which she, in her turn, appraised the Chief Superintendent.

This was the reason for Lapointe's uneasiness a little while back. The normal process of conducting a police inquiry with a view to apprehending a criminal was being overshadowed by the private duel between Maigret and this woman.

Nothing which did not directly concern her was of much interest to the Chief Superintendent. Lapointe was to have further proof of this when, a minute or two later, he came out of the telephone booth.

"What did he say?" asked Maigret, referring to Coméliau.

"He'll sign the warrant and send it across to your office."

"Does he want to see him?"

"He presumed you'd want to interrogate him first."

"What about her?"

"He's signing two warrants. It's up to you what you do with the second one, but if you ask me . . ."

"I see."

Coméliau was expecting Maigret to go back to

his office, and have Antoine and Madam Calas brought to him there separately, so that he could grill them for hours, until they gave themselves away.

The head of the dead man had still not been found. There was no concrete proof that the man whose remains had been fished out of the Saint-Martin Canal was Calas. All the same, they did now have strong circumstantial evidence, namely the suitcase, and it was by no means unusual to obtain a full confession, after a few hours of interrogation, in cases where the cards were more heavily stacked against the police.

Judge Coméliau was not the only one to see the matter in this light. Lapointe was of the same opinion, and he could scarcely hide his astonishment when Maigret instructed him: "Take him to Headquarters. Shut yourself up with him in my office, and get what you can out of him. Don't forget to order some food for him, and something to drink."

"Will you be staying here?"

"I'm waiting for Moers and the photographers."

Looking unmistakably put out, Lapointe motioned to the young man to stand up. As a parting shot, Antoine called to Maigret from the door:

"I warn you, you'll pay for this!"

At the Quai des Orfèvres, at about this time, the Vicomte, having poked his nose into most of the offices in the Palais de Justice, as he did every morning, had started on the Examining Magistrates.

"Any news, Monsieur Coméliau? Have they still not found the head?"

"Not yet. But I can tell you more or less officially that the identity of the victim is known."

"Who is it?"

Coméliau graciously consented to give ten minutes of his time to answering questions. He was not altogether displeased that, for once, it was he and not Maigret whom the press was honoring with its attentions.

"Is the Chief Superintendent still there?"

"I presume so."

Thus it came about that news of the inquiries in progress at the Calas bistro and the arrest of a young man, referred to only by his initials, appeared in the afternoon editions of the newspapers, two hours after the Vicomte's interview with Coméliau, and the five o'clock news on the radio included an announcement to the same effect.

Left on his own with Madame Calas, Maigret ordered a glass of wine at the bar, carried it across to a table, and sat down. As for her, she had not moved. She had remained at her post behind the bar where, as proprietress, she had every right to be.

The factory sirens sounded the midday break. In less than ten minutes, at least thirty people were crowded around the locked door. Some, seeing Madame Calas through the glass, indicated by gestures that they wanted to speak to her.

Suddenly, Maigret broke the silence.

"I've seen your daughter," he said.

She looked at him, but said nothing.

"She confirmed that she last came to see you about a month ago. I couldn't help wondering what you found to talk about."

It was not a question, and she did not choose to make any comment.

"She struck me as a sensible young woman, who

has done well for herself. I don't know why, but I had the feeling that she was in love with her boss, and might be his mistress."

Still she did not flinch. Was it of any interest to her? Did she feel any affection for her daughter, even the smallest remnant?

"It can't have been easy at the beginning. It's tough going for a girl of fifteen, trying to make her own way, alone, in a city like Paris."

She was still looking at him, but her eyes seemed to see through and beyond him. Wearily, she asked:

"What is it you want?"

What, indeed, did he want? Was Coméliau right after all? Ought he not to be engaged at this very moment in making Antoine talk? As for her, perhaps a few days in a police cell were just what was needed to bring about a change of heart.

"I'm wondering what made you marry Calas in the first place, and, even more, what induced you to stay with him all those years."

She did not smile, but the corners of her mouth twitched, in contempt, perhaps, or pity.

"It was done deliberately, wasn't it?" went on Maigret, not quite sure himself what he meant.

He had to get to the bottom of it. There were times, and this was one of them, when it seemed to him that he was within a hair's breadth not merely of solving the mystery but of sweeping aside the invisible barrier that stood between them. It was just a question of finding the words which would evoke the simple, human response.

"Was *the other one* here on Sunday afternoon?"

This, at least, did get results. She started. After a pause, she was reluctantly compelled to ask:

"What other one?"

"Your lover. Your real lover."

She would have liked to keep up the pretense of indifference, asking no questions, but in the end she yielded:

"Who?"

"A red-haired, middle-aged man, with smallpox scars, whose Christian name is Dieudonné."

It was as though a shutter had come down between them. Her face became completely expressionless. What was more, a car had drawn up at the door. Moers, and three men with cameras, had arrived.

Once again, Maigret went to the door and unlocked it.

Admittedly, he had not triumphed. All the same, he did not consider that their tête-à-tête had been altogether a waste of time.

"Where do you want us to search, sir?"

"Everywhere. The kitchen first, then the two rooms and the lavatory upstairs. There's the court-yard as well, and, of course, the cellar. This trap door here presumably leads to it."

"Do you believe the man was killed and dismembered here?"

"It's possible."

"What about this suitcase?"

"Go over it thoroughly. The contents too, of course."

"It will take us the whole afternoon. Will you be staying?"

"I don't think so, but I'll look in again later."

He went into the telephone booth and rang Judel at the Police Station opposite, to give him instructions about having the place watched.

When he had finished, he said to Madame Calas:

"You'd better come with me."

"Shall I take a change of clothing, and things for washing?"

"It would be advisable."

She stopped on her way through the kitchen for a stiff drink. Soon she could be heard moving about in the bedroom above.

"Is it safe to leave her on her own, sir?"

Maigret shrugged. If a crime had been committed here, steps must have been taken long before this to remove all traces of it, and dispose of anything incriminating.

All the same, it did surprise him that she should take so long getting ready. She could still be heard moving about, turning taps on and off, opening and shutting drawers.

She paused again in the kitchen, realizing no doubt that this was the last drink she would get for a long time.

When at last she reappeared, the men gaped at her in amazement, which in Maigret's case was mixed with a touch of admiration.

In the space of twenty minutes or less, she had completely transformed herself. She was now wearing a most becoming black coat. Under her carefully brushed hair and charming hat, her face seemed to have come to life. Her step was lighter, her carriage more upright. There was self-respect, even a hint of pride, in her bearing.

Was she aware of the sensation she was creating? Was there, perhaps, a touch of coquetry in her make-up? She did not smile, or show any sign of being amused at their astonishment. She looked inside her bag to make sure she had everything, and then, drawing on her gloves, said, almost in a whisper:

"I'm ready."

She was wearing face powder and lipstick. The scent of eau de Cologne, mingled with the fumes of brandy on her breath, seemed somehow inappropriate.

"Aren't you taking a suitcase?"

She said no, almost defiantly. Would it not be an admission of guilt to take a change of clothing? At the very least it would be an acknowledgment that there might be some justification for keeping her in custody.

"See you later!" Maigret called out to Moers and his assistants.

"Will you be taking the car?"

"No. I'll get a taxi."

It was a strange experience, walking by her side, in step with her, there in the sunlit street.

"The Rue des Récollets would be the best place to find a taxi, I imagine?"

"I expect so."

"I should like to ask you a question."

"You surprise me!"

"When did you last take the trouble to dress as you are dressed now?"

She looked thoughtful, obviously trying to remember.

"Four years ago or more," she said at last. "Why do you ask?"

"No particular reason."

What was the point of explaining, when she knew as well as he did? He managed to stop a taxi just as it was driving past. He opened the door for her, and got in beside her.

Chapter 6

The String

The truth was that he had not yet made up his mind what to do with her. If anyone but Judge Coméliau had been in charge of the case, things would have been different. He would have been prepared to take a risk. With Coméliau, it was dangerous. Not only was he finicky, a stickler for the rules, scared of public opinion and parliamentary criticism, but he had always mistrusted Maigret's methods, which he considered unorthodox. It had come to a head-on collision between them more than once in the past.

Maigret was well aware that the judge had his eye on him, and would not hesitate to hold him responsible if he were to step out of line or if anything, however trivial, should go wrong.

He would have much preferred to leave Madame Calas at the Quai de Valmy until he had a clearer insight into her character, and some clue as to her connection, if any, with the case. He would have posted a man, two men, to watch the bistro. But then Judel had posted a constable outside the tenement in the Faubourg Saint-Martin, and what good had that done? The boy Antoine had got away just the same. And Antoine was just an overgrown kid, with no more sense than a thirteen-year-old. Madame Calas was a different proposition. The newspapers in the kiosks already carried the story of the little café and its possible connection with the crime. At all events, Maigret had seen the name Calas in banner headlines on the front pages. Suppose, for instance, that tomorrow morning the headlines read: "Madame Calas disappears." He could just imagine his reception on arrival at the Judge's office.

While pretending to look straight before him, he was watching her out of the corner of his eye. She did not seem to notice. She was sitting up very straight, and there was an air of dignity about her. As they drove through the streets, she looked out of the window with interest and curiosity.

Just now she had admitted that she had not worn her street clothes for at least four years. She had not told him what the occasion was on which she had last worn her black dress. Perhaps it was even longer since she had been in the center of town, and seen the crowds thronging the Boulevards.

Since, on account of Coméliau, he was not free to do as he liked, he had had to adopt a different procedure.

As they were approaching the Quai des Orfèvres, the spoke for the first time.

"Are you sure you have nothing to tell me?"

She seemed a little taken aback.

"What about?"

"About your husband."

She gave a slight shrug, and said confidently:

"I didn't kill Calas."

She called him by his surname, as country women and shopkeepers' wives often call their husbands. But in her case it seemed to Maigret to strike a false note.

"Shall I drive up to the entrance?" the taxi driver turned around to ask.

"If you will."

The Vicomte was there, at the foot of the great staircase, in company with two other journalists and a number of photographers. They had got wind of what had happened, and it was useless to try to conceal the prisoner.

"One moment, Superintendent."

Did she imagine that Maigret had tipped them off? She held herself erect, as they took photographs, even following her up the stairs. Presumably Antoine, too, had undergone this ordeal.

They were upstairs in his own domain, and still Maigret had not made up his mind. In the end, he made for the Inspectors' Duty Room. Lucas was not there. He called to Janvier.

"Take her into an empty room for a few minutes and stay with her, will you?"

She could not help hearing. The Superintendent felt oppressed by the mute reproach of her look. Was it reproach, though? Was it not rather disillusionment?

He walked away without another word, and went to his own office, where he found his desk occupied by Lapointe, in shirt sleeves. Facing the window,

Antoine was sitting bolt upright in a chair, very flushed, as though he were feeling the heat.

Between them was the tray sent up from the Brasserie Dauphine. There were traces of beer in the two glasses, and a couple of half-eaten sandwiches on plates.

As Maigret's glance traveled from the tray to Antoine, he could see that the boy was vexed with himself for having succumbed. No doubt it had been his intention to "punish" them by going on hunger strike. They were familiar with self-dramatization in all its forms at the Quai des Orfèvres, and Maigret could not help smiling.

"How is it going?" he asked Lapointe.

Lapointe indicated, by a lift of the eyebrows, that he was getting nowhere.

"Carry on, boys."

Maigret went across to Comèliau's office. The magistrate was on his way out to lunch.

"Well, have you arrested the pair of them?"

"The young man is in my office. Lapointe is dealing with him."

"Has he said anything?"

"Even if he knows anything, he won't talk, unless we can prove something against him, and rub his nose in it."

"Is he a bright fellow?"

"That's exactly what he isn't. One can usually make an intelligent person see sense in the end, or at least persuade him to retract self-contradictory statements. An idiot will just go on denying everything, even in the teeth of the evidence."

"What about the woman?"

"I've left Janvier with her."

"Will you be dealing with her yourself?"

"Not for the moment. I haven't got enough to go on."

"When do you expect to be ready?"

"Tonight, maybe. If not, tomorrow or the next day."

"And in the meantime?"

Maigret's manner was so bland and amiable that Coméliau wondered what he was up to.

"I came to ask your advice."

"You can't keep her here indefinitely."

"That's what I think. A woman especially."

"Wouldn't the best thing be to have her locked up?"

"That's up to you."

"But you would prefer to let her go?"

"I'm not sure."

Frowning, Coméliau considered the problem. He was furious. Finally, as though he were throwing down a challenge, he barked:

"Send her to me."

"Why was the Chief Superintendent smiling as he disappeared down the corridor? Was it at the thought of a tête-à-tête between Madame Calas and the exasperated Judge?

He did not see her again that afternoon. He merely went into the Inspectors' Duty Room, and said to Torrence:

"Judge Coméliau wants to see Madame Calas. Let Janvier know, will you?"

The Vicomte intercepted him on the stairs. Maigret shook him off firmly, saying:

"Coméliau's the man you want to see. He'll be making a statement to the press, if not immediately then very shortly, you can take my word for it."

He stumped off to the Brasserie Dauphine, stopping at a bar for an apéritif. It was late. Almost everyone had had lunch. He went to the telephone.

"Is that you?" he said to his wife.

"Aren't you coming home?"

"No."

"Well, I hope you'll take time off for lunch."

"I'm at the Brasserie Dauphine. I'm just about to have something."

"Will you be home for dinner?"

"I may be."

The brasserie had its own distinctive blend of smells, among which two were dominant: the smell of Pernod around the bar, and that of coq-au-vin, which came in gusts from the kitchen.

Most of the tables in the dining room were unoccupied, though there were one or two of his colleagues lingering over coffee and Calvados. He hesitated, then went across to the bar and ordered a sandwich. The sun was still shining brilliantly, and the sky was clear, except for a few white clouds scudding across it. A sudden breeze had blown up, scattering the dust in the streets, and molding the women's dresses against their bodies.

The proprietor, behind the bar, knew Maigret well enough to realize that this was not the time to start a conversation. Maigret was eating absentmindedly, staring into the street with the mesmerized look of a passenger on board ship watching the monotonous and hypnotic motion of the sea.

"The same again?"

He said yes, probably not knowing what he had been eating, ate his second sandwich, and drank the coffee which was put in front of him before he had even ordered it.

A few minutes later he was in a taxi, heading

for the Quai de Valmy. He stopped it at the corner of the Rue des Récollets, opposite the lock, where three barges were lined up, waiting to go through. In spite of the filthy water whose surface was broken from time to time by unsavory-looking bubbles, there were a few anglers, tinkering with their floats as usual.

As he walked past Chez Popaul, with its yellow façade, the proprietor recognized him, and Maigret could see him, through the window, pointing him out to the people at the bar. All along the road, huge long-distant trucks were parked, bearing the name "Roulers and Langlois."

On his way, Maigret passed two or three little shops, of the sort to be found in all densely populated, residential districts of Paris. In front of one a trestle, piled high with fruit and vegetables, took up half the pavement. A few doors farther on, there was a butcher's shop which seemed to be empty, then, almost next door to Chez Calas, a grocer's shop, so dark that it was impossible to see into it.

Madame Calas must have had to go out sometimes, if only to do her marketing. These presumably were the shops she went to, wearing her slippers no doubt, and wrapped in the coarse, black, woolen shawl that he had noticed lying about in the café.

Judel must have interviewed the shopkeepers. The local police, being known to them, inspired more confidence than the men from the Quai des Orfèvres.

The door of the bistro was locked. He peered through the glass, but could see no one in the bar. Through the open kitchen door, however, he could see the flickering shadow of someone moving about

out of sight. He rapped his knuckles on the glass, but had to knock several times more before Moers appeared and, seeing him there, ran to unlock the door.

"I'm sorry. We were making quite a lot of noise. Have you been waiting long?"

"It doesn't matter."

It was he who remembered to lock the door again.

"Have you had many interruptions?"

"Most people try the door and then go away, but some are more persistent. They bang on the door, and go through a whole pantomime to be let in."

Maigret looked around the room, then went behind the bar to see if he could find a blotting pad, like the one advertising an apéritif that he had seen on the table in the in the bedroom. There were usually several of these blotters dotted about in cafés, and it struck him as odd that here there was not even one, though the place was well supplied with other amenities, including three games of dominoes, four or five bridge cloths, and half-a-dozen packs of cards.

"You carry on," he said to Moers. "I'll be back shortly."

He threaded his way through the cameras set up in the kitchen, and went upstairs, returning with the bottle of ink and the blotting pad.

He sat down at a table in the café, and wrote in block capitals:

"CLOSED UNTIL FURTHER NOTICE."

He paused after the first word, thinking perhaps of Coméliau closeted at this very minute with Madame Calas.

"Are there any thumbtacks anywhere?"

Moers answered from the kitchen:

"On the left-hand side of the shelf under the counter."

He found them, and went out to pin his notice above the door. Coming back, he felt something brush against his leg, something alive, and looked down to see the ginger cat gazing up at him and mewing.

That was something he had overlooked. If the place was going to be left unoccupied for any length of time, something would have to be done about the cat.

He went into the kitchen, and found some milk in an earthenware jug, and a cracker soup plate.

"Who can I get to look after the cat?"

"Wouldn't a neighbor take it? I noticed a butcher's shop on my way here."

"I'll see about it later. Anything interesting, so far?"

They were going through the place with a fine-tooth comb, sifting through the contents of every drawer, searching every corner. First Moers, examining things under a magnifying glass or, when necessary, his portable microscope, then the photographers, recording everything on film.

"We began with the courtyard, because, with all the junk there is out there, it seemed the most likely place to choose if one had something to hide."

"I take it the trash baskets have been emptied since Sunday?"

"On Monday morning. All the same, we examined them thoroughly, especially for traces of blood."

"Nothing?"

121

"Nothing," repeated Moers, after a moment's hesitation.

Which meant that he thought he might be on to something, but was not sure.

"What is it?"

"I don't know, sir. It's just an impression that all four of us had. We were discussing it when you arrived."

"Go on."

"Well, there's something peculiar about the set-up, at least as far as the courtyard and the kitchen are concerned. This isn't the sort of place you'd expect to find spotlessly clean. You only have to open a few drawers to see that everything is stuffed in anyhow, and most of the things are thick with dust."

Maigret looked about him. He saw what Moers meant, and his eyes brightened with interest.

"Go on."

"There was a three days' pile of dirty dishes on the draining board, and several saucepans. There's been no washing up done since Sunday. An indication of slovenly habits, you might think. Unless it's just that the woman lets things slide when her husband's away."

Moers was right. She wouldn't bother to keep the place tidy, or even particularly clean.

"In other words, one would expect to find dirt everywhere, dirt accumulated over a period of a week or ten days. In fact, in some drawers and inaccessible corners, we did find dirt that had been there even longer. In general, however, there was evidence that the place had been recently and extensively scrubbed, and Sambois found a couple of bottles of bleach in the courtyard, one of them empty and, judging from the condition of the label, recently bought."

"When would you say this spring cleaning had been done?"

"Three or four days ago. I can't be more definite until I've made one or two tests in the lab, but I should know for certain by the time I come to write my report."

"Any fingerprints?"

"They bear out our theory. Calas's prints are all over the drawers and cupboard, only on the inside, though."

"Are you sure?"

"Well, at any rate, they are the same as those of the body in the canal."

Here, at last, was proof that the dismembered corpse was that of the proprietor of the bistro in the Quai de Valmy.

"What about upstairs?"

"Nothing on the surface, only inside the wardrobe door and so on. Dubois and I have only been up there to look around. We'll make a thorough job of it later. What struck us was that there wasn't a speck of dust on any of the furniture, and that the floor had been thoroughly scrubbed. As for the bed, the sheets were changed recently, probably three or four days ago."

"Were there dirty sheets in a laundry basket, or anywhere else?"

"I thought of that. No."

"Was the washing done at home?"

"I couldn't see any evidence of it. No washing machine or tub."

"So they must have used a laundry?"

"I'm almost sure of it. So unless the truck called yesterday or the day before . . ."

"I'd better try and find out the name of the laundry. The neighbors will probably know."

But before the words were out of Maigret's mouth, Moers had gone over to the dresser and opened one of the drawers.

"Here you are."

He handed Maigret a bundle of bills, some of which bore the heading: "Récollets Laundry." The most recent was ten days old.

Maigret went into the telephone booth, dialed the number of the laundry, and asked whether any washing had been collected from the bistro that week.

"We don't call at the Quai de Valmy until Thursday morning," he was told.

So that last collection of laundry had been on the previous Thursday.

No wonder it had struck Moers as odd. Two people do not live in a house for almost a week without soiling some household linen. Where was it, then, and in particular where were the dirty sheets? The ones on the bed had certainly not been there since Thursday.

He was looking thoughtful when he went back to join the others.

"What was it you were saying about the prints?"

"So far, in the kitchen, we have found prints belonging to three people, excluding yourself and Lapointe, whose prints I know by heart. The prints most in evidence are a woman's. I presume they're Madame Calas's."

"That can easily be checked."

"Then there are the prints of a man, a young man

124

I should guess. There aren't many of them, and they are the most recent."

Antoine, presumably, for whom Madame Calas must have got a meal in the kitchen when he turned up in the middle of the night.

"Finally, there are two prints, half obliterated. Another man's."

"Any more of Calas's prints inside the drawers?"

"Yes."

"In other words, it looks as though very recently, on Sunday possibly, someone cleaned the place from top to bottom, but didn't bother with turning out drawers and cupboards?"

They were all thinking of the dismembered corpse, which had been recovered piecemeal from the canal.

The operation could not have been undertaken in the street or on open ground. It must have taken time, and each part had been carefully wrapped in newspaper, and tied with string.

What would any room look like, after being used for such a purpose?

Maigret's remorse at having delivered Madame Calas into the merciless clutches of Judge Coméliau was beginning to subside.

"Have you been down to the cellar?"

"We've been everywhere, just to get our bearings. At a glance, everything looked quite normal down there, but there again, we'll be going over it thoroughly later."

He left them to get on with their work, and spent some time in the café roaming about, with the ginger cat following him like a shadow. The bottles on the shelf reflected the sun, and there were warm pools of light on the corner of the bar counter. He remembered the great stove in the middle of the room, and wondered whether it had gone out. He looked inside, and saw that there were still a few glowing embers. Mechanically, he stroked it up.

Next, he went behind the counter, studied the bottles, hesitated, and then poured himself a glass of Calvados. The drawer of the till was open. It was empty except for a couple of notes and some small change. The list of drinks and prices was posted near the window to his right.

He consulted it, took some loose change out of his pocket, and dropped the money for the Calvados into the till. Just then he caught sight of a figure beyond the glass door, and gave a guilty start. It was Inspector Judel peering in.

Maigret went to unlock the door.

"I thought you'd probably be here, sir. I rang Headquarters, but they didn't seem to know where you'd gone."

Judel looked around, and seemed surprised at the absence of Madame Calas.

"Is it true, then, that you have arrested her?"

"She's with Judge Coméliau."

Judel caught sight of the technicians at work in the kitchen, and jerked his chin in their direction.

"Have they found anything?"

"It's too early to say."

And it would take too long to explain. Maigret could not face it.

"I'm glad I found you here, because I didn't want to take action without your authority. I think we've found the man with red hair."

"Where?"

"If my information is correct, practically next door. Unless, that is, he's on night shift this week.

126

He's a warehouse man with Zenith Transport, the firm . . ."

"Rue des Récollets. I know. Roulers and Langlois."

"I thought you would wish to interview him yourself."

Moers called from the kitchen:

"Can you spare a minute, sir?"

Maigret went over to the door at the back of the café. Madame Calas's black shawl was spread out on the kitchen table, and Moers, having already examined it through his magnifying glass, was focusing his microscope.

"Take a look at this."

"What is it I'm supposed to see?"

"You see the black wool fibers, and those brownish threads like twigs, intertwined with them? Well in fact, those are strands of hemp. It will have to be confirmed by analysis, of course, but I'm quite sure in my own mind. They're almost invisible to the naked eye, and they must have rubbed off onto the shawl from a ball of string."

"The same string that . . . ?"

Maigret was thinking of the string used to tie up the remains of the dismembered man.

"I could almost swear to it. I don't imagine Madame Calas very often had occasion to tie up a parcel. There are several kinds of string in one of the drawers, thin white string, red string, and twine, but not a scrap of string anything like this."

"I'm much obliged to you. I take it you'll still be here when I get back?"

"What are you going to do about the cat?"

"I'll take it with me."

Maigret picked up the cat, which did not seem to

mind, and carried it outside. He considered entrusting it to the grocer, but decided that it would probably be better off with the butcher.

"Isn't that Madame Calas's cat?" asked the woman behind the counter, when he went in with it.

"Yes. I wonder if you'd mind looking after it for a few days?"

"So long as it doesn't fight with my own cats."

"Is Madame Calas a customer of yours?"

"She comes in every morning. Is it really her husband who . . . ?" When it came to putting such a grisly question into words, she balked, and could only look toward the canal.

"It looks like it."

"What's to become of her?"

And before Maigret could fob her off with an evasive answer, she went on:

"Not everyone would agree with me, I know, and there are plenty of grounds for fault-finding, but I think she's a poor, unhappy creature, and, whatever she's done, she was driven to it."

A few minutes later, Maigret and Judel were in the Rue des Récollets, waiting for a break in the stream of trucks leaving the depot, to cross over safely to the forecourt of Roulers and Langlois. They went to the glass box on the right, on which the word "Office" was inscribed in block letters. All around the forecourt were raised platforms, like those in a railway freight yard, piled high with boxes, sacks, and crates, which were being loaded onto the trucks. People were charging about, heavy packages were being roughly manhandled. The noise was deafening.

Maigret had his hand on the doorknob when he heard Judel's voice behind him:

"Sir!"

The Superintendent turned around to see a red-haired man standing on one of the platforms, with a narrow logbook in one hand and a pencil in the other. He was staring intently at them. He was broad-shouldered, of medium height, and wearing a gray overall. He was fair-skinned with a high color, and his face, pitted with smallpox scars, had the texture of orange rind. Porters loaded with freight were filing past him, each in turn calling out a name and number, followed by the name of a town or village, but he did not seem to hear them. His blue eyes were fixed upon Maigret.

"See that he doesn't give us the slip," said Maigret to Judel.

He went into the office, where the girl at the inquiry desk asked him what she could do for him.

"I'd like to speak to someone in authority."

There was no need for her to reply. A man with close-cropped, gray hair came forward to find out what he wanted.

"Are you the manager?"

"Joseph Langlois. Haven't I seen you somewhere before?"

No doubt he had seen Maigret's photograph in the papers. The Chief Superintendent introduced himself, and Langlois waited in uneasy silence for him to explain his business.

"Who is that red-haired fellow over there?"

"What do you want him for?"

"I don't know yet. Who is he?"

"Dieudonné Pape. He's been with us for over twenty-five years. It would surprise me very much if you'd got anything against him."

"Is he married?"

"He's been a widower for years. In fact, I believe his wife died only two or three years after their marriage."

"Does he live alone?"

"I suppose so. His private life is no concern of mine."

"Have you got his address?"

"He lives in the Rue des Ecluses-Saint-Martin, very near here. Do you remember the number, Mademoiselle Berthe?"

"Fifty-six."

"Is he here all day, every day?"

"He puts in his eight hours, like everyone else, but not always in the daytime. We run a twenty-four-hour service here, and there are trucks loading and unloading all through the night. This means working on a three-shift system, and the rota is changed everyweek."

"What shift was he on last week?"

Langlois turned to the girl whom he had addressed as Mademoiselle Berthe.

"Look it up, will you?"

She consulted a ledger.

"The early shift."

The boss interpreted:

"That means, he came on at six in the morning and was relieved at two in the afternoon."

"Is the depot open on Sundays as well?"

"Only with a skeleton staff. Two or three men."

"Was he on duty last Sunday?"

The girl once more consulted the ledger.

"No."

"What time does he come off duty today?"

"He's on the second shift, so he'll be off at ten tonight."

"Could you arrange to have him relieved?"

"Can't you tell me what all this is about?"

"I'm afraid that's impossible."

"Is it serious?"

"It may be very serious."

"What is he supposed to have done?"

"I can't answer that."

"Whatever you may think, I can tell you here and now that you're barking up the wrong tree. If all my staff were like him, I shouldn't have anything to worry about."

He was far from happy. Without telling Maigret where he was going or inviting him to follow, he strode out of the glass-walled office and, skirting the trucks in the forecourt, went over to Dieudonné Pape.

The man stood motionless and expressionless, listening to what his boss had to say, but his eyes never left the glass box opposite. Langlois went to the storage shed, and seemed to be calling to someone inside, and indeed, within seconds, a little old man appeared, wearing an overall like Pape, with a pencil behind his ear. They exchanged a few words, and then the newcomer took the narrow log-book from the red-haired man, who followed the boss around the edge of the forecourt.

Maigret had not moved. The two men came in, and Langlois loudly announced:

"This is a Chief Superintendent from Police Headquarters. He wants a word with you. He thinks you may be able to help him."

"I have one or two question to ask you, Monsieur Pape. If you'll be good enough to come with me."

Dieudonné Pape pointed to his overall.

"Do you mind if I change?"

"I'll come with you."

Langlois did not see the Superintendent out. Maigret followed the warehouse man into a sort of corridor that served as a cloakroom. Pape asked no questions. He was in his fifties, and seemed a quiet, reliable sort of man. He put on his hat and coat, and, flanked on the right by Judel and on the left by Maigret, walked to the street.

He seemed surprised that there was no car waiting for them outside, as though he had expected to be taken straight to the Quai des Orfèvres. When, on the corner opposite the yellow façade of Chez Popaul, they turned not right toward the town center, but left, he seemed about to speak, but then apparently though better of it, and said nothing.

Judel realized that Maigret was making for the Calas bistro. The door was still locked. Maigret rapped on the glass. Moers came to let them in.

"In here, Pape."

Maigret turned the key.

"You know this place pretty well, don't you?"

The man looked bewildered. If he had been expecting a visit from the police, he had certainly not expected this.

"You may take off your coat. We've kept the fire going. Take a seat, in your usual place if you like. I suppose you have your own favorite chair?"

"I don't understand."

"You're a regular visitor here, aren't you?"

"I'm a customer, yes."

Seeing Moers and his men in the kitchen with their cameras, he peered, trying to make out what was going on. He must have been wondering what had happened to Madame Calas.

"A very good customer?"

132

"A good customer."

"Were you here on Sunday?"

He had an honest face, with a look in his blue eyes that was both gentle and timid. Maigret was reminded of the way some animals look when a human being speaks sharply to them.

"Sit down."

He did so, cowering, because he had been ordered to do so.

"I was asking you about Sunday."

He hesitated before answering: "I wasn't here."

"Were you at home all day?"

"I went to see my sister."

"Does she live in Paris?"

"Nogent-sur-Marne."

"Does she have a telephone?"

"Nogent three-one-seven. She's married to a builder."

"Did you see anyone besides your sister?"

"Her husband and children. Then, at about five, the neighbors came in for a game of cards, as usual."

Maigret made a sign to Judel, who nodded and went to the telephone.

"What time was it when you left Nogent?"

"I caught the eight o'clock bus."

"You didn't call in here before going home?"

"No."

"When did you last see Madame Calas?"

"On Saturday."

"What shift were you on last week?"

"The early shift."

"So it was after two when you got here?"

"Yes."

133

"Was Calas at home?"

Again, he hesitated.

"Not when I came in."

"But he was, later?"

"I don't remember."

"Did you stay long in the café?"

"Quite a time."

"How long would that be?"

"Two hours, at least. I can't say exactly."

"What did you do?"

"I had a glass of wine, and we talked for a bit."

"You and the other customers?"

"No, I talked mostly to Aline."

He flushed as he spoke her name, and hurriedly explained:

"I look upon her as a friend. I've known her for a long time."

"How long?"

"More than ten years."

"So you've been coming here every day for ten years?"

"Almost every day."

"Preferably, when her husband was out?"

This time he did not reply. He hung his head, troubled.

"Are you her lover?"

"Who told you that?"

"Never mind. Are you?"

Instead of replying, he asked anxiously:

"What have you done with her?"

And Maigret told him outright:

"She's with the Examining Magistrate at the moment."

"Why?"

"To answer a few questions about her husband's disappearance. Don't you read the papers?"

As Dieudonné Pape sat motionless, lost in thought, Maigret called out:

"Moers! Take his prints, will you?"

The man submitted quietly, appearing more anxious than frightened, and his fingertips, pressed down on the paper, were steady.

"See if they match."

"Which ones?"

"The two in the kitchen. The ones you said were partly rubbed out."

As Moers went out, Dieudonné Pape, gently reproachful, said:

"If all you wanted to know was whether I had been in the kitchen, you only had to ask me. I often go in there."

"Were you there last Saturday?"

"I made myself a cup of coffee."

"What do you know about the disappearance of Omer Calas?"

He was still looking very thoughtful, as though he were hesitating on the brink of some momentous decision.

"Didn't you know he'd been murdered, and his dismembered corpse thrown into the canal?"

It was strangely moving. Neither Judel nor Maigret had been prepared for it. Slowly, the man turned toward the Superintendent, and gave him a long, searching look. At last he said, gently reproachful still:

"I have nothing to say."

Maigret, looking as serious as the man he was questioning, pressed him:

"Did you kill Calas?"

And Dieudonné Pape, shaking his head, repeated:

"I have nothing to say."

Chapter 7

The Cat

Maigret was finishing his meal when he became
aware of the way his wife was looking at him, with
a smile that was maternal and yet, at the same time,
a little teasing. At first, pretending not to notice, he
bent over his plate, and ate a few more spoonfuls
of his custard. But he could not help looking up in
the end:

"Have I got a smut on the end of my nose?" he
asked grumpily.

"No."

"Then why are you laughing at me?"

"I'm not laughing. I'm smiling."

"You're making fun of me. What's so comical
about me?"

"There's nothing comical about you, Jules."

She seldom called him "Jules"; only when she
was feeling protective toward him.

"What is it, then?"

"Do you realize that during the entire dinner you haven't said a single word?"

No, he had not realized it.

"Have you any idea what you've been eating?"

Assuming a fierce expression, he said:

"Sheep's kidneys."

"And before that?"

"Soup."

"What kind of soup?"

"I don't know. Vegetable soup, I suppose."

"Is it because of that woman you've got yourself into such a state?"

Most of the time, and this was a case in point, Madame Maigret knew no more about her husband's work than she read in the newspapers.

"What is it? Don't you believe she killed him?"

He shrugged, as though he were carrying a burden and wished he could shake it off.

"I just don't know."

"Or that Dieudonné Pape did it with her as his accomplice?"

He was tempted to reply that it was of no consequence. Indeed, as he saw it, this was not the point. What mattered to him was understanding what lay behind the crime. As it was, not only was this not yet clear to him, but the more he knew of the people involved, the more he felt himself to be floundering.

He had come home to dinner instead of staying in his office to work on the case, for the very reason that he needed to get away from it, to return to the jog-trot of everyday life, from which he had hoped to go back with sharpened perceptions to the protagonists in the Quai de Valmy drama. Instead, as his wife had teasingly pointed out, he had sat through dinner without opening his mouth, and continued to think of nothing but Madame Calas and Pape, with the boy, Antoine, thrown in for good measure.

It was unusual for him to feel at this stage that he was still a long way from a solution. But then, in this case, the problems were not amenable to police methods.

Murders in general can be classified under a few broad headings, three or four at most.

The apprehension of a professional murderer is only a matter of routine. When a Corsican gangster strikes down a gangster from Marseilles in a bar in the Rue de Douai, the police have recourse to standard procedures, almost as though tackling a problem in mathematics.

When a couple of misguided youths commit robbery with violence, injuring or killing an old woman in a tobacconist's shop, or a bank clerk, it may be necessary to pursue the assailants through the streets, and here too there is a standard procedure.

As to the *crime passionnel*, nothing could be more straightforward. With murder for financial gain, through inheritance, life insurance, or some more devious means, the police know themselves to be on solid ground as soon as they have discovered the motive.

Judge Coméliau, for the present, was inclined to the view that financial gain was the motive in the Calas case, perhaps because he was incapable of accepting the idea that anyone outside his own social sphere, especially people from a neighborhood like the Quai de Valmy, could have any but the crudest motives.

Given that Dieudonné Pape was the lover of

Madame Calas, Dieudonné Pape and Madame Calas must have got rid of the husband, partly because he was an encumbrance, and partly to get hold of his money.

"They have been lovers for ten years or more," Maigret had objected. "Why should they have waited all that time?"

The magistrate had brushed this aside. Maybe Calas had recently come into possession of a substantial sum of money. Maybe the lovers had been waiting for a convenient opportunity. Maybe there had been a row between Madame Calas and her husband, and she felt she had put up with enough. Maybe . . .

"And suppose we find that, except for the bistro, which isn't worth much, Calas had nothing?"

"The bistro is something. Dieudonné may have got fed up with his job with Zenith Transport, and decided that he would prefer to end his days dozing in front of the fire in his carpet slippers in a cozy little café of his own."

Here, Maigret had to concede, was a possibility, even though remote.

"And what about Antoine Cristin?"

The fact was that the Judge was now saddled not with one suspect but two. Cristin too was Madame Calas's lover, and if anyone was likely to be short of money, it was he rather than Pape.

"The other two were just making use of him. You'll find that he was their accomplice, mark my words."

This, then, was the official view—or at least the view prevailing in one examining magistrate's office —of the Quai de Valmy affair. Meanwhile, until the real facts were brought to light, all three of them were being kept under lock and key.

Maigret was the more disgruntled in that he reproached himself for not having stood up to Coméliau. Owing to indolence perhaps, or cowardice, he had given in without a struggle.

At the outset of his career, he had been warned by his superiors always to be sure of his ground before putting a suspect through a rigorous cross-examination, and experience had confirmed the wisdom of this advice. A properly conducted cross-examination did not consist in drawing a bow at a venture, or hurling accusations at a suspect for hours on end, in the hope that he would break down and confess.

Even a half-wit has a kind of sixth sense, which enables him to recognize at once whether the police are making accusations at random or have solid grounds for suspicion.

Maigret always preferred to bide his time. On occasion, in cases of real difficulty, he had even been willing to take a risk rather than arrest a suspect prematurely.

And he had been proved right every time.

"Contrary to popular belief," he was fond of saying, "being arrested can be something of a relief to a suspected person, because, from then on, he does at least know where he stands. He no longer has to ask himself: 'Am I under suspicion? Am I being followed? Am I being watched? Is this a trap?' He has been charged. He can now speak in his own defense. And henceforth he will be under the protection of the law. As a prisoner, he has his rights, hallowed rights, and nothing will be done to him which is not strictly in accordance with the rules."

Aline Calas was a case in point. From the moment she had crossed the magistrate's threshold, her lips had, as it were, been sealed. Coméliau had got no more out of her than if she had been the gravel in the hold of the Naud brothers' barge.

"I have nothing to say," was all she would utter, in her flat, expressionless voice.

And when he persisted in bombarding her with questions, she retorted:

"You have no right to question me, except in the presence of a lawyer."

"In that case, kindly tell me the name of your lawyer."

"I have no lawyer."

"Here is the membership list of the Paris Bar. You may take your choice."

"I don't know any of them."

"Choose a name at random."

"I have no money."

There was therefore no choice but for the Court to nominate counsel for her, and that was a slow and cumbersome process.

Late that afternoon, Coméliau had sent for Antoine who, having held out against hours of questioning by Lapointe, saw no reason to be more forthcoming with the magistrate.

"I did not kill Monsieur Calas. I didn't go to the Quai de Valmy on Sunday afternoon. I never handed in a suitcase at the checkroom of the Gare de l'Est. Either the clerk is lying or he's made a mistake."

All this time, his mother, red-eyed, clutching a crumpled handkerchief, sat waiting in the lobby at Police Headquarters. Lapointe had tried to reason with her, and, after him, Lucas. It was no good. She was determined to wait, she repeated over and over again, until she had seen Chief Superintendent Maigret.

She was a simple soul, who believed, like many of her kind, that it was no good talking to underlings. She must, at all costs, see the man at the top.

The Chief Superintendent could not have seen her then, even if he had wanted to. He was just laving the bar in the Quai de Valmy, accompanied by Judel and Dieudonné Pape.

"Don't forget to lock up, and bring the key to Headquarters," he said to Moers.

The three men crossed by the footbridge to the Quai de Jemmapes, only a few yards from the Rue ds Ecluses-Saint-Martin, behind the Hospital of Saint-Louis. It was a quiet neighborhood, more provincial than Parisian in character. Pape was not handcuffed. Maigret judged that he was not the man to make a run for it. His bearing was calm and dignified, not unlike that of Madame Calas herself. He looked sad rather than shocked, and seemed withdrawn, or was it resigned?

He said very little. He had probably never been a talkative man. He answered, when spoken to, as briefly as possible. Sometimes he did not answer at all, but just looked at the Chief Superintendent out of his lavender-blue eyes.

He lived in an old five-story building, which had an appearance of respectability and modest comfort.

As they passed the lodge, the concierge got up and peered at them through the glass. They did not stop, however, but went up to the second floor. Pape went to a door on the left, and opened it with his key.

There were three rooms in the apartment: bedroom, dining room, and kitchen. There was also a large store-cupboard converted into a bathroom. It surprised Maigret to see that there was a well-equipped bathroom. The furniture, though not new, was less old-fashioned than that of the house in the Quai de Valmy, and everything was spotlessly clean.

"Do you have a daily woman?" Maigret asked in surprise.

"No."

"You mean you do your own housework?"

Dieudonné Pape could not help smiling with gratification. He was proud of his home.

"Doesn't the concierge ever give you a hand?"

There was a meat-safe, fairly well stocked with provisions, on the kitchen window sill.

"Do you do your own cooking as well?"

"Always."

Above the sideboard in the dining room hung a large gilt-framed photograph of Madame Calas, so much like those commonly to be seen in the houses of respectable families of modest means that it lent an air of cozy domesticity to the room.

Recalling that not a single photograph had been found at the Calases', Maigret asked:

"How did you come by it?"

"I took it myself, and had the enlargement made somewhere in the Boulevard Saint-Martin."

His camera was in the sideboard drawer. On a small table in a corner of the bathroom, there were a number of glass dishes and bowls and several bottles of developing fluid.

"Do you do much photography?"

"Yes. Landscapes and buildings, mostly."

It was true. Going through the drawers, Maigret

found a large number of views of Paris, and a few landscapes. There were a great many of the canal and the Seine. Judging from the striking effects of light and shade in most of the photographs, it must have cost Dieudonné Pape a great deal in time and patience to get the shots he wanted.

"What suit were you wearing when you went to your sister's?"

"The dark blue."

He had three suits, including the one he was wearing.

"We shall need those," Maigret said to Judel, "and the shoes."

Then, coming upon some soiled underclothes in a wicker basket, he added them to the rest.

He had noticed a canary hopping about in a cage, but it was not until they were leaving the apartment that it occurred to him that it would need looking after.

"Can you think of anyone who might be willing to take care of it?"

"The concierge would be only too pleased, I'm sure."

Maigret fetched the cage and took it to the lodge. The concierge came to the door before he had time to knock.

"You're surely not taking him away!" she exclaimed in a fury.

She meant her tenant, not the canary. She recognized Judel, who was a local man. Possibly she recognized Maigret, too. She had read the newspapers.

"How dare you treat him like a criminal! He's a good man. You couldn't hope to find a better."

She was a tiny little thing, of gipsy complexion

and sluttish appearance. Her voice was shrill, and she was so enraged that it would not have surprised him if she had sprung at him and tried to scratch his eyes out.

"Would you bewilling to look after the canary for a short time?"

She literally snatched the cage out of his hand.

"Just you wait and see what the tenants and all the other people round here will have to say about this! And for a start, Monsieur Dieudonné, we'll all be coming to see you in prison."

Elderly working-class women quite often hero-worship bachelors and widowers of Dieudonné Pape's type, whose well-ordered way of life they greatly admire. The concierge followed the three men onto the pavement, and stood there sobbing and waving to Pape.

Maigret turned to Judel:

"Give the clothes and the shoes to Moers. He'll know what to do. And I want the bistro kept under surveillance."

In giving instructions that a watch should be kept on the bistro, he had nothing particular in mind. It was just to cover himself if anything were to go wrong. Dieudonné Pape waited obediently on the edge of the pavement, and then fell into step with Maigret, as they walked alongside the canal in search of a taxi.

He was silent in the taxi, and Maigret decided not to question him further. He filled his pipe, and held it out to Pape.

"Do you smoke a pipe?"

"No."

"Cigarette?"

"I don't smoke."

146

Maigret did, after all, ask Pape a question, but it had, on the face of it, nothing to do with the death of Calas.

"Don't you drink either?"

"No."

Here was another anomaly. Maigret could not make it out. Madame Calas was an alcoholic. She had been drinking for years, presumably even longer than she had know Pape.

As a rule, a compulsive drinker cannot endure the companionship of a teetotaler.

The Chief Superintendent had encountered couples very like Madame Calas and Dieudonné Pape before. In every case, as far as he could remember, both the man and the woman drank.

He had been brooding abstractedly over this at dinner, unaware that his wife was watching him. And that was not all, by any means. Among other things, there was Antoine's mother, whom he had found waiting in the lobby at the Quai des Orfèvres. Handing Pape over to Lucas, he had taken her into his office.

He had not forgotten to instruct Lucas to let Coméliau know that Pape had been brought in:

"If he wants to see him, take him there. Otherwise, take him to the cells."

Pape, poker-faced, had gone with Lucas into an office, while Maigret led the woman away.

"I swear to you, Superintendent, that my son would never do a thing like that. He couldn't hurt a fly. He makes himself out to be a tough guy because it's the thing at his age. But I know him, you see. He's just a child."

"I'm sure you're right, Madame."

"In that case, why don't you let him go? I'll keep

147

him indoors from now on, and there won't be any more women, I promise you. That woman is almost as old as I am! She ought to know better than to take up with a fellow young enough to be her son. It's shameful! I've known for some time that there was something going on. When I saw he was buying hair cream, brushing his teeth twice a day, and even using scent, I said to myself . . ."

"Is he your only child?"

"Yes. And I've always taken extra care of him, on account of his father having died of consumption. I did everything I could for him, Superintendent. If only I could see him! If only I could talk to him! Surely they won't try to stop me? They wouldn't keep a mother from her son, would they?"

There was nothing he could do but pass her on to Coméliau. He knew it was cowardly, but he really had no choice. Presumably she had been kept waiting all over again, up there in the corridor, on a bench. Maigret did not know whether or not the Judge had finally granted her an interview.

Moers had got back to the Quai des Orfèvres just before six, and handed Maigret the key of the house in the Quai de Valmy. It was a heavy, old-fashioned key. Maigret put it in his pocket with the key to Pape's apartment.

"Did Judel give you the clothes and the shoes?"

"Yes, I've got them in the lab. It's blood we're looking for, I suppose?"

"Mainly, yes. I may want you to look over his apartment tomorrow morning."

"I'll be working here late tonight, after I've had a bite to eat. It's urgent, I imagine?"

It always was urgent. The longer a case dragged

on, the colder the scent, and the more time for the criminal to cover his tracks.

"Will you be in tonight?"

"I don't know. In any case, you'd better leave a note on my desk on your way out."

He got up from the table, filling his pipe, and looked uncertainly at his armchair. Seeing him so restless, Madame Maigret ventured:

"Why not give yourself a rest for one night? Put the case out of your mind. Read a book, or, if you'd rather, take me to the movies. You'll feel much fresher in the morning."

With a quizzical look, he said:

"Do you want to see a movie?"

"There's quite a good program at the Moderne."

She poured his coffee. He could not make up his mind. He felt like taking a coin out of his pocket and tossing for it.

Madame Maigret was careful not to pursue the subject, but sat with him while he slowly sipped his coffee. He paced up and down the dining room, taking long strides, only pausing from time to time to straighten the carpet.

"No!" he said at last, with finality.

"Will you be going out?"

"Yes."

He poured himself a small glass of sloe gin. When he had drunk it, he went to get his overcoat.

"Will you be home late?"

"I'm not sure. Probably not."

Perhaps because he had a feeling that he was about to take a momentous step, he did not take a taxi or ring the Quai des Orfèvres to order a police car. He walked to the Métro station and boarded a train for Château-Landon. He felt again the disturbing night-time atmosphere of the place, with ghostly figures lurking in the shadows, women loitering on the pavements, and the bluish-green lighting in the bars making them look like fish-tanks in an aquarium.

A man standing a few yards from the door of Chez Calas saw Maigret stop, came straight up to him, and shone a flashlight in his face.

"Oh! Sorry, sir. I didn't recognize you in the dark."

It was one of Judel's constables.

"Anything to report?"

"Nothing. Or rather there is one thing. I don't know if it's of any significance. About an hour ago, a taxi drove past. It slowed down about fifty yards from here and went by at a crawl, but it didn't stop."

"Could you see who was in it?"

"A woman. I could see her quite clearly under the gas lamp. She was young, wearing a gray coat and no hat. Farther down, the taxi gathered speed and turned left into the Rue Louis-Blanc."

Was it Madame Calas's daughter, Lucette, come to see whether her mother had been released? She must know, from the newspaper reports, that she had been taken to the Quai des Orfèvres, but no further details had been released.

"Do you think she saw you?"

"Very likely. Judel didn't tell me to stay out of sight. Most of the time, I've been walking up and down to keep warm."

Another possible explanation was that Lucette Calas had intended to go into the house, but changed her mind when she saw that it was being watched. If that were the case, what was she after?

He shrugged, took the key out of his pocket, and

fitted it into the lock. He had some difficulty in finding the light switch, which he had not had occasion to use until now. A single light came on. The switch for the light at the far end of the room was behind the bar.

Moers and his assistants had put everything back in its proper place before leaving, so that there was no change in the little café, except that it felt colder, because the fire had been allowed to go out.

On his way to the kitchen, Maigret was startled to see something move. He had not heard a sound, and it took him seconds to realize that it was the cat, which he had left with the butcher earlier in the day.

The creature was rubbing its back against his legs now, and Maigret, bending down to stroke it, growled:

"How did you get in?"

It worried him. The back door, leading from the kitchen to the courtyard, was bolted, and the window was closed too. He went upstairs, turned on the light, and found that a window had been left open. There was a lean-to shed, with a corrugated iron roof, in the back yard of the house next door. The cat must have climbed onto it, and taken a flying leap over a gap of more than six feet.

Maigret went back down the stairs. Finding that there was a drop of milk left in the earthenware jug, he poured it out for the cat.

"What now?" he said aloud, as though he were addressing the animal.

They certainly made an odd pair, alone in the empty house.

He had never realized how deserted, even desolate, a bar could look with no one behind the counter and not a customer in sight. Yet this was how the place must have looked every night after everyone had gone, and Monsieur and Madame Calas had put up the shutters and locked the door.

There would be just the two of them, man and wife, with nothing left to do but put out the lights and go upstairs to bed. Madame Calas, after all those nips of brandy, would be in her usual state of vacant torpor.

Did she have to conceal her drinking from her husband? Or did he take an indulgent view of his wife's addiction to the bottle, seeking his own pleasures elsewhere in the afternoons?

Maigret suddenly realized that there was one character in the drama about whom almost nothing was known, the dead man himself. From the outset, he had been to all of them merely a dismembered corpse. It was an odd fact that the Chief Superintendent had often noticed before, that people did not respond in the same way to parts of a body found scattered about as to a whole corpse. They did not feel pity in the same degree, or even revulsion. It was as though the dead person were somehow dehumanized, almost an object of ridicule.

He had never seen Calas's face, even in a photograph, and the head had still not been found, and probably never would be.

The man was of peasant stock, short and squat in build. Every year he went to the vineyards near Poitiers to buy his wine. He wore good suits, and played billiards in the afternoon, somewhere near the Gare de l'Est.

Other than Madame Calas, was there a woman in his life, or more than one perhaps? Could he possibly have been aware of what went on when he was away from home?

He had accidentally encountered Pape, and, unless he were crassly insensitive, he must have seen how things stood between Pape and his wife.

The impression they created was not so much of a pair of lovers as of an old married couple, united in a deep and restful contentment, born of mutual understanding, tolerance, and that special tenderness which, in the middle-aged, is often a sign that much has been forgiven and forgotten.

Had he known all this, and accepted it philosophically? Had he turned a blind eye or, alternatively, had there been scenes between him and his wife?

And what about the others who, like Antoine, were in the habit of slinking in to take advantage of Aline Calas's weakness? Had he known about them too, and if so, how had he taken it?

Maigret was back behind the bar, his hand hovering over the bottles on the shelf. In the end he took down a bottle of Calvados, reminding himself that he must leave the money for it. The cat had gone over to the stove, but instead of dozing as it usually did, was restless, bewildered to find no heat coming from it.

Maigret understood the relationship between Madame Calas and Pape. He also understood the role of Antoine and the casual callers.

What he did not understand at all was the relationship between Calas and his wife. How and why had those two ever come together, subsequently married, and lived with one another for so many years? And what about their daughter, in whom neither of them seemed to have taken the slightest interest, and who appeared to have nothing whatever in common with them?

There was nothing to enlighten him, not a single photograph or letter, none of those personal possessions which reveal so much about their owners.

He drained his glass, and grumpily poured himself another drink. Then, with the glass in his hand, he went and sat at the table where he had seen Madame Calas sitting, with that settled air which suggested that it was her usual place.

He tapped out his pipe against his shoe, refilled it and lit it. He stared at the bar counter, the glasses and bottles, and the feeling came over him that he was on the brink of a revelation. Maybe it would not answer all his questions, but it would answer some of them at least.

What kind of home was this, after all, with its kitchen where no food was served, since the Calases ate their meals at a table in a corner of the café, and its bedroom which was only used to sleep in?

Whichever way you looked at it, this was their real home, this bar, which was to them what the dining room or living room is to an ordinary family.

Was it not the case that on their arrival in Paris, or very soon after, they had settled here in the Quai de Valmy, and remained ever since?

Maigret was smiling now. He was beginning to understand Madame Calas's relationship with her husband, and more than this, to see where Dieudonné Pape came into it.

It was very vague still, and he would not have been able to put it into words. All the same, there was no denying that he has quite shaken off his earlier mood of indecision. He finished his drink, went into the telephone booth, and dialed the number of the Central Police Station.

"Chief Superintendent Maigret speaking. Who is

that? Oh! It's you, Joris. How is your new arrival getting on? Yes, I do mean the Calas woman. What's that? Oh! What are you doing about it?"

It was pitiful. Twice she had called for the guard, and each time she had begged him to get her something to drink. She was willing to pay anything, anything at all. Maigret had not foreseen the terrible suffering that this deprivation would cause her.

"No, of course not . . ."

It was not possible for him to suggest to Joris that he should give her a drink in breach of the regulations. Perhaps he himself could take her a bottle in the morning, or have her brought to his office and order something for her there?

"I'd like you to look through her papers for me. She must have been carrying an identity card. I know she comes from somewhere round about Gien, but I can't remember the name of the village."

He was kept waiting some time.

"What's that? Boissancourt-par-Saint-André. Boissancourt with an a? Thanks, old man. Good night! Don't be too hard on her."

He dialed Directory Inquiries, and gave his name.

"Would you be so kind, Mademoiselle, as to find the directory for Boissancourt-par-Saint-André—between Montargis and Gien—and read out the names of the subscribers."

"Will you hold on?"

"Yes."

It did not take long. The supervisor was thrilled at the prospect of collaborating with the celebrated Chief Superintendent Maigret.

"Shall I begin?"

"Yes."

"Aillevard, Route des Chênes, occupation not stated."

"Next."

"Ancelin, Victor, butcher. Do you want the number?"

"No."

"Honoré de Boissancourt, Château de Boissancourt."

"Next."

"Doctor Camuzet."

"I'd better have his number."

"Seventeen."

"Next."

"Calas, Robert. Cattle dealer."

"Number?"

"Twenty-one."

"Calas, Julien, grocer. Number: three."

"Any other Calas?"

"No. There's a Louchez, occupation not stated, a Piedboeuf, blacksmith, and a Simonin, corn dealer."

"Will you please get me the first Calas on the list. I may want the other later."

He heard the operator talking to the intermediate exchanges, then a voice saying:

"Saint-André Exchange."

Boissancourt-par-Saint-André 21 was slow to answer. At last, a woman's voice said:

"Who's speaking?"

"Chief Superintendent Maigret here, from Police Headquarters, Paris. Are you Madama Calas? Is your husband at home?

He was in bed with influenza.

"Have you a relative by the name of Omer Calas?"

"Oh, him! What's happened to him? Is he in trouble?"

"Do you know him?"

"Well, I've never actually met him. I don't come from these parts. I'm from the Haute-Loire district, and he left Boissancourt before my marriage."

"Is he related to your husband?"

"They're first cousins. His brother is still living here. Julien. He owns the grocer's shop."

"Can you tell me anything more about him?"

"About Omer? No, I don't know any more. What's more I don't want to."

She must have hung up, because another voice was asking:

"Shall I get the other number, Superintendent?"

There was less delay this time. A man's voice answered. He was even more uncommunicative.

"I can hear you perfectly well. But what exactly do you want from me?"

"Are you the brother of Omer Calas?"

"I did have a brother called Omer."

"Is he dead?"

"I haven't the least idea. It's more than twenty years, nearer twenty-five, since I last heard anything of him."

"A man by the name of Omer Calas has been found murdered in Paris."

"So I heard just now on the radio."

"Then you must have heard his description—does it fit your brother?"

"It's impossible to say after all this time."

"Did you know he was living in Paris?"

"No."

"Did you know he was married?"

Silence.

"Do you know his wife?"

"Now, look here, there's nothing I can tell you. I was fifteen when my brother left home. I haven't seen him since. He's never written to me. I just don't want to know. I'll tell you who might be able to help you: Maître Canonge."

"Who is he?"

"The notary."

When, at last, he got through to Maître Canonge's number, a woman's voice, that of Madame Canonge, exclaimed:

"Well, of all the extraordinary coincidences!"

"I beg your pardon?"

"That you should call at this moment! How did you know? Just now, when we heard the news on the radio, my husband was of two minds whether to get in touch with you by telephone or go to Paris and see you. In the end, he decided to make the journey, and he caught the eight twenty-two train, which is due in at the Gare d'Austerlitz shortly after midnight. I'm not certain of the exact time."

"Where does he usually stay in Paris?"

"Until recently the train went on to the Gare d'Orsay. He always stayed at the Hôtel d'Orsay, and still does."

"What does your husband look like?"

"Good-looking, tall and well-built, with gray hair. He's wearing a brown suit and overcoat. He has his brief-case with him, and a pigskin suitcase. I still can't imagine what made you think of phoning him!"

Maigret put down the receiver with an involuntary smile. Things were going so well that he considered treating himself to another drink, but thought better of it. There would be plenty of time to have one at the station.

But first, he must ring Madame Maigret, and tell her that he would be late getting home.

Chapter 8

The Notary

Madame Canonge had spoken no more than the truth. Her husband really was a fine-looking man. He was about sixty, and in appearance more like a gentleman farmer than a country lawyer. Maigret, waiting at the end of the platform near the barrier, picked him out at once. He stood head and shoulders above the other passengers on the 12:22 train, and walked with a rapid stride, his pigskin suitcase in one hand and his brief-case in the other. His air of easy assurance suggested that he knew his way about and was probably a regular traveler on this particular train. Maigret noted all this when he was still quite a long way off.

Added to his height and impressive build, his clothes set him apart from the other passengers. He was almost too well dressed. To describe his coat as brown was to do less than justice to its color,

which was a soft, subtle chestnut such as Maigret
had never seen before, and the cut was masterly.

His fresh complexion was set off by silvery hair,
and even in the unflattering light of the station
entrance he looked well groomed, smooth shaven,
the kind of man whom one would expect to complete
his toilet with a discreet dab of eau de Cologne.

When he was within fifty yards of the barrier,
he caught sight of Maigret among the other people
meeting the train, and frowned as though trying
to recapture an elusive memory. He, too, must often
have seen the Chief Superintendent's photograph in
the newspapers. Even when he was almost level
with Maigret, he was still too uncertain to smile or
hold out his hand.

It was Maigret who stepped forward to meet him.

"Maître Canonge?"

"Yes. Aren't you Chief Superintendent Maigret?"

He put down his suitcase and shook Maigret's
hand.

"It can't be just a coincidence that I should find
you here, surely?"

"No. I telephoned your house earlier this evening.
Your wife told me that you were on this train, and
would be staying at the Hôtel d'Orsay. I thought it
advisable, for security reasons, to meet the train
rather than ask for you at your hotel."

The notary looked puzzled.

"Did you see my advertisement?"

"No."

"You don't say! The sooner we get out of here
the better, don't you think? I suggest we adjourn
to my hotel."

They got into a taxi.

"The reason I'm here is to see you. I intended to call you first thing tomorrow morning."

Maigret had been right. There was a faint fragrance of eau de Cologne blended with the lingering aroma of a good cigar.

"Have you arrested Madame Calas?"

"Judge Coméliau has signed the warrant."

"What an extraordinary business!"

It was a short journey along the quayside to the Hôtel d'Orsay. The night porter greeted Maître Canonge with the warmth due to a guest of long standing.

"The restaurant is shut, I suppose, Alfred?"

"Yes, sir."

The notary explained to Maigret, who knew the facts perfectly well:

"Before the war, when the Quai d'Orsay was the terminus for all trains on the Paris-Orléans line, the station restaurant was open all night. It was very convenient. A hotel bedroom isn't the most congenial place in the world. Wouldn't it be better if we talked over a drink somewhere?"

Most of the brasseries in the Boulevard Saint-Germain were closed. They had to walk quite a distance before they found one open.

"What will you have, Superintendent?"

"A beer, thanks."

"And a brandy for me, waiter, the best you have."

Having left their coats and hats in the cloakroom, they sat at the bar. Maigret lit his pipe, and Canonge pierced a cigar with a silver penknife.

"I don't suppose you know Saint-André at all?"

"No."

"It's miles from anywhere, and there are no

162

tourist attractions. If I'm not mistaken, according to the afternoon news bulletin, the man who was carved up and dropped in the Saint-Martin Canal was none other than that swine Calas."

"Fingerprints of the dead man were found in the house in the Quai de Valmy."

"When I first read about the body in the canal, although the newspapers hadn't much to say about it then, I had a kind of intuition, and I toyed with the idea of phoning you even then."

"Did you know Calas?"

"I knew him in the old days. I knew her better, though—the woman who became his wife, I mean. Cheers! The trouble is, I hardly know where to begin, it's all so involved. Has Aline Calas never mentioned me?"

"No."

"Do you really think she's involved in the murder of her husband?"

"I don't know. The examining magistrate is convinced of it."

"What has she to say about it?"

"Nothing."

"Has she confessed?"

"No. She refuses to say anything."

"To tell you the truth, Chief Superintendent, she's the most extraordinary woman I've ever met in my life. And, make no mistake, we have our fair share of freaks in the country."

He was clearly accustomed to a respectful audience, and he liked the sound of his own voice. He held his cigar in his elegant fingers in such a way as to show off his gold signet ring to the best advantage.

"I'd better begin at the beginning. You'll never

have heard of Honoré de Boissancourt, of course?"

The Superintendent shook his head.

"He is, or rather was until last month, the 'lord of the manor.' He was a rich man. Besides the Château de Boissancourt, he owned some fifteen farms comprising five thousand acres in all, plus another two and a half thousand acres of woodland and two small lakes. If you are at all familiar with country life, you can visualize it."

"I was born and brought up in the country."

And what was more, Maigret's father had been farm manager on just such an estate.

"Now I think you ought to know something of the antecedent of this fellow, Boissancourt. It all began with his grandfather. My father, who, like myself, practiced law in Saint-André, knew him well. He wasn't called Boissancourt, but Dupré, Christophe Dupré, son of a tenant farmer whose landlord was the former owner of the château. Christophe began by dealing in cattle, and he was sufficiently ruthless and crooked to amass a considerable fortune in a short time. You know his sort, I daresay."

To Maigret, it was as though he were reliving his own childhood, for his village had had its Christophe Dupré, and he too had amassed great wealth, and had a son who was now a senator.

"At one stage, Dupré speculated heavily in wheat, and the gamble paid off. With what he made on the deal, he bought one farm, then a second and a third, and by the end of his life the château and all the land attached to it, which had been the property of a childless widow, had passed into his hands. Christophe had one son and one daughter. The daughter he married off to cavalry officer. The son,

Alain, came into the property on his father's death, and used the name of Dupré de Boissancourt. Gradually the Dupré was dropped and, when he was elected to the County Council, he changed his name by deed poll."

This, too, evoked memories for Maigret.

"Well, so much for the antecedents. Honoré de Boissancourt, the grandson of Christophe Dupré, who was, as it were, the founder of the dynasty, died a month ago.

"He married Emilie d'Espissac, daughter of a fine old family who had fallen on hard times. There was one daughter of this marriage. The mother was killed in a riding accident, when the child was only a baby. I knew Emilie well. She was a charming woman, though no beauty. She sadly underrated herself, and allowed her parents to sacrifice her, without protest. It was said that Boissancourt gave the parents a million francs, by way of purchase price one must assume. As the family lawyer, I am in a position to know that the figure was exaggerated, but the fact remains that a substantial sum of money came into the possession of the old Comtesse d'Espissac as soon as the marriage contract was signed."

"What kind of man was Honoré?"

"I'm coming to that. I was his legal adviser. For years, I have been in the habit of dining at the château once a week, and I've shot over his land ever since I was a boy. In other words, I know him well. In the first place, he had a clubfoot, which may explain his moody and suspicious disposition. Then again, his family history was known to everyone, and most of the county families refused to have anything to do with him. None of this was exactly calculated to bring out the best in him.

"All his life he was obsessed with the notion that people despised him, and were only out to cheat and rob him. He was forever on the defensive.

"There is a turret room in the château, which he used as a kind of office. He spent days on end up there, going through the accounts, not only those of his tenants, but all the household bills as well, down to the last penny. He made all his corrections in red ink. He would poke his nose into the kitchen at mealtimes, to make sure that the servants weren't eating him out of house and home.

"I suppose I owe some loyalty to my client, but it's not as if I were betraying a professional secret. Anyone in Saint-André could tell you as much."

"Was he the father of Madame Calas?"

"Exactly."

"What about Omer Calas?"

"He was a servant at the château for four years. His father was a drunken laborer, a real bum.

"Which brings us to Aline de Boissancourt, as she was twenty-five years ago."

He signaled to the waiter as he went past the table, and said to Maigret:

"Join me in a brandy this time, won't you? Two *fines champagnes,* waiter."

Then, turning back to the Superintendent, he went on:

"Needless to say, you couldn't possibly have any inkling of her background, seeing her for the first time in the bistro in the Quai de Valmy."

This was not altogether the case. Nothing that the notary had told Maigret was any surprise to him.

"Old Doctor Petrelle used sometimes to talk to

me about Aline. He's dead now, unfortunately, and Camuzet has taken over the practice. Camuzet never knew her, so he wouldn't be any help. And I myself am not qualified to describe her case in technical terms.

"Even as a very young child, she was different from other little girls. There was something disturbing about her. She never played with other children, or even went to school, because her father insisted on keeping her at home with a governess. Not one governess, actually, but at least a dozen, one after the other, because the child somehow contrived to make their lives a misery.

"Was it that she blamed her father for the fact that her life was so different from other children's? Or was there, as Petrelle believed, much more to it than that? I don't know. It's often said that girls worship their fathers, sometimes to an unnatural degree. I can't speak from my own experience. My wife and I have no children. But is it possible, I wonder, for that kind of adoration to turn into hatred?

"Be that as it may, she seemed prepared to go to any lengths to drive Boissancourt to distraction, and at the age of twelve she was caught setting fire to the château.

"She was always setting fire to things at that time, and she had to be kept under strict supervision.

"And then there was Omer. He was five or six years older than she was, tough and strong, a 'likely lad' as country folk say, and as insolent as you please as soon as the boss's back was turned."

"Did you know what was going on between them?" inquired Maigret, looking vaguely round

167

the brasserie, which was now almost empty, with the waiters obviously longing for them to go.

"Not at the time. I heard about it later from Petrelle. According to him, when she first began taking an interest in Omer she was only thirteen or fourteen. It's not unusual in girls of that age, but as a rule it's just calf love, and nothing comes of it.

"Was it any different in her case? Or was it just that Calas, who wasn't the kind to allow his better feelings to stand in his way, was more unscrupulous in taking advantage of her than most men would be in a similar situation?

"Petrelle, at any rate, was convinced that their relationship was suspect right from the start. In his opinion, Aline had only one idea in her head, to defy and wound her father.

"It may be so. I'm not competent to judge. I'm only telling you all this, because it may help you to understand the rest of the story.

"One day, when she was not yet seventeen, she went to see the doctor in secret, and asked him to examine her. He confirmed that she was pregnant."

"How did she take it?" asked Maigret.

"As Petrelle described it, she gave him a long, hard look, clenched her teeth, and spat out the words:

" '*I'm glad!*'

"I should tell you that Calas, meanwhile, had married the butcher's daughter. She was pregnant too, of course, and their child was born a few weeks earlier.

"He carried on with his job at the château, not being fitted for any other work, and his wife went on living with her parents.

"It was a Sunday when the news burst upon the

village that Aline de Boissancourt and Omer Calas had vanished.

"It was learned from the servants that, the night before, there had been a violent quarrel between the girl and her father. They could hear them in the breakfast room, going at it hammer and tongs for over two hours.

"Boissancourt, to my certain knowledge, never made any attempt to find his daughter. And, as far as I know, she never communicated with him.

"As for Calas's first wife, she suffered from fits of depression. She dragged on miserably for three years. Then, one day, they found her hanging from a tree in the orchard."

The waiters by now had stacked most of the chairs on the tables, and one of them was looking fixedly at Maigret and the notary, with a large silver pocket watch in his hand.

"I think we'd better be going," suggested Maigret.

Canonge insisted on paying the bill, and they went out into the cool, starlit night. They walked a little way in silence. Then the notary said:

"What about a nightcap, if we can find a place that's still open?"

Each wrapped in his own thoughts, they walked almost the whole length of the Boulevard Raspail, and eventually, in Montparnasse, found a little cabaret which appeared to be open, judging from the bluish light shining into the street, and the muffled sound of music.

"Shall we go in?"

They did not follow the waiter to a table, but sat at the bar. The fat man next to them was more than a little drunk, and was being pestered by a couple of prostitutes.

"The same again?" asked Canonge, taking another cigar out of his pocket.

There were a few couples dancing. Two prostitutes came across from the far end of the room to sit beside them, but they melted away at a sign from Maigret.

"There are still Calases at Boissancourt and Saint-André," remarked the notary.

"I know. A cattle dealer and a grocer."

Canonge sniggered:

"Suppose the cattle dealer were to grow rich in his turn, and buy the château and the land for himself. What a laugh that would be! One of the Calases is Omer's brother, the other is his cousin. There is a sister as well. She married a policeman in Gien. A month ago, just as he was sitting down to his dinner, Boissancourt dropped dead of a cerebral hemorrhage. I went to see all three of them in the hope that one or the other might have news of Omer."

"Just a moment," interposed Maigret. "Didn't Boissancourt disinherit his daughter?"

"Everyone in the district was convinced that he had. There was a good deal of speculation as to who would inherit the property, because, in a village like ours, most people are more or less dependent on the château for their livelihood."

"You knew, I daresay."

"No. Boissancourt made several wills over the past few years, all different, but he never deposited any of them with me. He must have torn them up, one after another, because no will was found."

"Do you mean to say his daughter inherits everything?"

"Automatically."

"Did you put a notice in the papers?"

"Routinely, yes. There was no mention of the name Calas, because I couldn't assume that they were married. Not many people read that kind of advertisement. I didn't think anything would come of it."

His glass was empty, and he was trying to catch the barman's eye. There had evidently been a restaurant car on the train, and he must have had a couple of drinks before reaching Paris, because he was very flushed, and his eyes were unnaturally bright.

"The same again, Superintendent?"

Maigret, too, had perhaps had more to drink than he realized. He did not say so. He was feeling fine, physically and mentally. It seemed to him, in fact, that he had acquired a sixth sense, enabling him to penetrate the mysteries of human personality. Had he really needed the notary to fill in the details? Might he not, in the end, have worked the whole thing out for himself? He had not been far from the truth a few hours earlier. Why else should he have put that call through to Saint-André?

Even if he had not dotted the *i*'s and cross the *t*'s, the impression he had formed of Madame Calas had been very close to the truth. All that he had been told confirmed this.

"She's taken to drink," he murmured, prompted by a sudden urge to have his say.

"I know. I've seen her."

"When? Last week?"

This was another thing that he had worked out for himself. But Canonge would not let him get a word in edgewise. In Saint-André, no doubt, he was used to holding forth without interruption.

"All in good time, Superintendent. I'm a lawyer,

remember, and in legal circles matters are dealt with in their correct order."

He guffawed at this. A prostitute sitting at the bar leaned across the unoccupied stool between them, and said:

"Won't you buy me a drink?"

"If you like, my dear, but you mustn't interrupt. You might not think it, but we are discussing weighty matters."

Mightily pleased with himself, he turned to Maigret.

"Well, now, for three weeks there was no answer to my advertisement, other than a couple of letters from cranks. And, in the end, it wasn't the advertisement that led me to Aline. It was pure chance. I had sent one of my guns to a firm in Paris for repair, and last week I got it back. It came through a firm of long-distance truckers. I happened to be at home when it was delivered. In fact, I opened the door myself."

"And the truckers were Zenith Transport?"

"How did you know? You're quite right. I invited the driver in for a drink, as one does in the country. Calas's grocery store is just opposite my house in the Place de l'Eglise. We can see it from our front windows. The man was having his drink when he suddenly noticed the name over the shop:

" 'Would that be the same family as the people who have the bistro in the Quai de Valmy?' he said, half to himself.

" 'Is there a Calas in the Quai de Valmy?'

" 'It's a funny little place. I'd never set foot in it until last week, when I was taken there by one of the warehouse men.' "

Maigret was willing to take a bet that this warehouse man was none other than Dieudonné Pape.

"He didn't happen to say whether the warehouse man had red hair?"

"No. I asked him if he knew the Christian name of this Calas. He thought about it for a bit, and then said he vaguely remembered seeing it over the door. I asked, could it be Omer, and he said yes, that was it.

"At any rate, next day, I left by train for Paris."

"The night train?"

"No. The morning train."

"What time did you go to the Quai de Valmy?"

"In the afternoon, shortly after three. The bistro is rather dark, and when I first saw the woman, I didn't recognize her. I asked her if she was Madame Calas, and she said she was. Then I asked her Christian name. I got the impression that she was half drunk. She does drink, doesn't she?"

So did he drink, not as she did, but enough, all the same, to make his eyes water now.

Maigret had an uneasy feeling that they had just had their glasses refilled, but he was not too sure. The woman had moved to the stool next to the notary, and was lolling against him with her arm through his. For all the expression on her face, she might not have heard a word of what he had said.

" 'Your maiden name was Aline de Boissancourt, is that right?' I said.

"She didn't deny it. She just sat there by the stove, staring at me, I remember, with a great ginger cat on her lap.

"I went on:

" 'Your father is dead. Did you know?'

"She shook her head—no sign of surprise or emotion.

" 'As his lawyer, I am administering his estate. Your father left no will, which means that the château, the land, and all he possessed come to you.'

" 'How did you get my address?' she asked.

" 'From a truck driver who happened to have been in here for a drink.'

" 'Does anyone else know?'

" 'I don't think so.'

"She got up and went into the kitchen."

To take a swig from the brandy bottle, of course!

"When she got back, I could see that she had come to some decision.

" 'I don't want anything to do with the money,' she said, as though it was of no importance. 'I suppose I can refuse it if I want to?'

" 'Everyone has the right to renounce an inheritance. Nevertheless . . .'

" 'Nevertheless what?'

" 'I would advise you to think it over. Don't make up your mind here and now.'

" 'I've thought it over. I refuse it. I imagine I also have the right to insist that you keep your knowledge of my whereabouts to yourself.'

"All the while she was talking she kept peering nervously into the street, as though she were afraid someone would come in, her husband, perhaps. That's what I thought, at any rate.

"I protested, as I was bound to do. I told her I hadn't been able to trace anyone else with a claim to the Boissancourt estate.

" 'Perhaps it would be best for me to come back another time and talk things over again.' I suggested.

" 'No. Don't come back. Omer mustn't see you here. I won't have it.'

"She was terrified.

" 'It would be the end of everything!' she said.

" 'Don't you think you ought to consult your husband?'

" 'He's the very last person!'

"I tried to argue with her, but it was no use. As I was leaving, I gave her my card. I said that, if she changed her mind in the next few weeks, she could telephone or write, and let me know.

"A customer came in then. He looked to me very much at home in the place."

"Red-haired, with a pock-marked face?"

"Yes, I believe he was!"

"What happened?"

"Nothing. She slipped my card into her apron pocket, and saw me to the door."

"What day was it?"

"Last Thursday."

"Did you see her again?"

"No. But I saw her husband."

"In Paris?"

"In my study at home, in Saint-André."

"When?"

"On Saturday morning. He arrived in Saint-André on Friday afternoon or evening. He first called at the house on Friday evening, about eight. I was out, playing bridge at the doctor's house. The maid told him to come back next day."

"Did you recognize him?"

"Yes, although he had put on weight. He must have spent the night at the village inn, where, of course, he learned that Boissancourt was dead. He must also have heard that his wife was heir to the property. He lost no time in throwing his weight about. He insisted that, as her husband, he was entitled to claim the inheritance in the name of his wife. As there was no marriage contract in this case, the joint-estate system applies."

"So that, in fact, neither could act without the consent of the other?"

"That's what I told him."

"Did you get the impression that he had discussed the matter with his wife?"

"No. He didn't even know that she had renounced the inheritance. He seemed to think she'd got hold of it behind his back. I won't go into the details of the interview, it would take too long. What must have happened is that he found my card. His wife probably left it lying around. Very likely she forgot I'd given it to her. And what possible business would a lawyer from Saint-André have in the Quai de Valmy unless it were to do with the de Boissancourt estate?

"It was only while he was talking to me that the truth gradually dawned on him. He was furious. I should be hearing from him, he said, and stormed out, slamming the door."

"And you never saw him again?"

"I never heard another word from him. All this happened on Saturday morning. He went by bus to Montargis, and caught the train to Paris from there."

"What train would that be, do you think?"

"Probably the one that gets in at the Gare d'Austerlitz just after three."

Which meant that he must have arrived at about four, or earlier if he took a taxi.

The notary went on:

"When I read about the dismembered body of a

man recovered from the Saint-Martin Canal, right there next to the Quai de Valmy, it shook me, I can tell you. I couldn't help being struck by the coincidence. As I said just now, I was in two minds about calling you, but I didn't want to look like a fool.

"It was when I heard the name Calas mentioned in the news this afternoon that I made up my mind to come and see you."

"Can I have another?" asked the girl next to him, pointing to her empty glass.

"By all means, my dear. Well, what do you think, Superintendent?"

At the word "Superintendent," the prostitute started, and let go of the notary's arm.

"It doesn't surprise me," murmured Maigret, who was beginning to feel drowsy.

"Come now, don't tell me you've ever known anything like it! Things like that only happen in the country, and I must say that even I . . ."

Maigret was no longer listening. He was thinking of Aline Calas, whom he was now able to see in the round. He could even imagine her as a little girl.

He was not surprised or shocked. He would have found it hard to explain what he felt about her, especially to a man like Judge Coméliau. On that score, he had no illusions; he would be listened to tomorrow with amazement and disbelief.

Coméliau would protest:

"They killed him just the same, she and that lover of hers."

Omer Calas was dead, and he certainly had not taken his own life. Someone, therefore, had struck him down, and subsequently dismembered his body.

Maigret could almost hear Coméliau's acid voice:

"What can you call that but cold-blooded? You can't imagine, surely, that it was a *crime passionnel?* No, Maigret, you've talked me around before, but this time . . ."

Canonge held up his brimming glass:

"Cheers!"

"Cheers!"

"You look very thoughtful."

"I was thinking about Aline Calas."

"Do you think she took up with Omer just to spite her father?"

Even to the notary, even under the influence of several glasses of brandy, he could not put his feelings into words. For a start, he would have to convince him that everything she had done, even as a kid in the Château de Boissancourt, had been a kind of protest.

Doctor Petrelle, no doubt, would have been able to express it better than he could. To begin with, the fire setting; then, her sexual relations with Calas, and finally, her flight with him in circumstances in which most other girls would have procured an abortion.

This too, perhaps, had been an act of defiance? Or revulsion?

Maigret had often tried to persuade others, men of wide experience among them, that, of all people, those most likely to come to grief, to seek self-abasement and degradation with morbid fervor, almost with relish, are the idealists.

To no avail. Coméliau would protest:

"If you said she was born wicked, you'd be nearer the truth."

At the bistro in the Quai de Valmy, she had taken to drink. This, too, was in character. And so was the fact that she had remained there without ever attempting to escape, allowing the atmosphere of the place to engulf her.

Maigret believed he understood Omer too. It was the dream of so many country boys to earn enough money in domestic service, or as a chauffeur, to become the proprietor of a bistro in Paris. For Omer the dream had come true.

It was a life of ease, lounging behind the bar, shuffling down to the cellar, going to Poitiers once or twice a year to buy wine, spending every afternoon playing billiards or *belote* in a brasserie near the Gare de l'Est.

There had not been time to investigate his private life. Maigret intended to go into that in a day or so, if only to satisfy his own curiosity. He was convinced that, when he was not indulging his passion for billiards, Omer had had a succession of shameless affairs with local servant girls and shop assistants.

Had he counted on inheriting the Boissancourt property? It seemed unlikely. He must have believed, like everyone else, that de Boissancourt had disinherited his daughter.

It had taken the notary's visiting card to arouse his hopes.

"I've had to do with all sorts in my time," Canonge was saying, "but what I simply can't understand—indeed, I confess it's quite beyond me, my dear fellow—is how, with a fortune landing in her lap out of the blue, she could bring herself to turn it down."

To Maigret, however, it seemed perfectly natural. As she was now, what possible use could she make of the money? Go and live with Omer in the Château

179

de Boissancourt? Set up house with him in Paris or elsewhere—the Côte d'Azur for instance—in the style of rich landowners?

She had chosen to stay where she was, in the place where she felt safe, like an animal in its lair.

Day had followed day, all alike, punctuated by swigs of brandy behind the kitchen door, and Dieudonné Pape's company in the afternoons.

He too had become a habit, more than a habit, perhaps, because he knew. She need not feel ashamed with him. They could sit side by side in companionable silence, warming themselves by the stove.

"Do you believe she killed him?"

"I don't think so."

"It was her lover, then?"

"It looks like it."

The musicians were putting away their instruments. Even this place had to close sometime. They found themselves outside in the street, walking in the direction of Saint-Germain-des-Prés.

"How far do you have to go?"

"Boulevard Richard-Lenoir."

"I'll walk with you part of the way. What could have induced the lover to kill Omer? Was he hoping to persuade her to change her mind about the estate?"

They were both unsteady on their feet, but quite up to roaming the streets of Paris, which they had to themselves but for an occasional passing taxi.

"I don't think so."

He would have to take a different tone tomorrow with Coméliau. At the moment, he suddenly realized, he was sounding quite maudlin.

"Why did he kill him?"

"What would you say was the first thing Omer would do when he got back from Saint-André?"

"I don't know—lose his temper, I imagine, and order his wife to accept the inheritance."

Maigret saw again the table in the bedroom, the bottle of ink, the blotter, and the three sheets of blank paper.

"That would be in character, wouldn't it?"

"No doubt about it."

"Supposing Omer ordered her to write a letter to that effect, and she still refused?"

"He'd have thrashed her. He was that sort—a real peasant."

"He did resort to violence on occasion."

"I think I can see what you're getting at."

"He doesn't bother to change when he gets home. This is Saturday afternoon, around four. He marches Aline up to her room, orders her to write the letter, uses threatening language, and starts knocking her about."

"At which point the lover shows up?"

"It's the most likely explanation. Dieudonné Pape knows his way about the house. He hears the row in the bedroom, and rushes upstairs to Aline's rescue."

"And does the husband in!" finished the notary, with a snigger.

"He kills him, either deliberately or accidentally, by hitting him on the head with something heavy."

"After which, he chops him up!"

Canonge, who was distinctly merry, roared with mirth.

"It's killing!" he exclaimed. "I can't help laughing at the thought of anyone carving up Omer. I mean to say, if you'd known Omer ..."

Far from sobering him up, the fresh air, on top of all he had drunk, had gone to his head.

"Do you mind walking back with me part of the way?"

They faced about, walked a little way, and then turned back again.

"He's a strange man," murmured Maigret, with a sigh.

"Who? Omer?"

"No, Pape."

"Don't tell me he's called Pape, on top of everything else!"

"Not just Pape, Dieudonné Pape."

"Killing!"

"He's the mildest man I've ever met."

"No doubt that's why he chopped up poor old Omer!"

It was perfectly true. It took a man like him, self-sufficient, patient, meticulous, to remove all traces of the crime. Not even Moers and his men, for all their cameras and apparatus, had been able to find any proof that a murder had been committed in the house on the Quai de Valmy.

Had Aline Calas helped him scrub the place from top to bottom? Was it she who had got rid of the sheets and clothes, with their tell-tale stains?

Pape had slipped up in one particular: he had not foreseen that Maigret would be puzzled by the absence of dirty linen in the house, and would make inquiries of the laundry. But how could he have foreseen that?

How had those two imagined their future? Had they believed that weeks, possibly months, would elapse before any part of Calas's body was found in the canal, and that by then, it would be beyond identification? That was what would have happened if the Naud brothers' barge had not been weighed down by several extra tons of gravel, and scraped the bottom of the canal.

Where was the head? In the river? In a drain? Maigret would probably know the answer in a day or two. Sooner or later, he was convinced, he would know everything there was to know, but it was of merely academic interest to him. What mattered to him was the tragedy and the three protagonists who had enacted it, and he was certain he was right about them.

Aline and Pape, he felt sure, once all traces of the murder had been eradicated, had looked forward to a new life, not very different from the old.

For a while, things would have gone on as before, with Pape coming into the little café every afternoon for a couple of hours. Gradually, he would have spent more and more time there. In time, the neighbors and customers would have forgotten Omer Calas, and Pape would have moved in altogether.

Would Aline have continued to receive Antoine Cristin and the other men in the kitchen?

It was possible. On this subject, Maigret did not care to speculate. He felt out of his depth.

"It really is good night, this time!"

"Can I phone you tomorrow at your hotel? There are various formalities to be gone through."

"No need to ring me. I shall be in your office at nine."

Needless to say, the notary was not in Maigret's office at nine, and Maigret had forgotten that he had said he would be. The Superintendent was not feeling any too bright. This morning, in response to a touch on the shoulder from his wife, he had opened his eyes, with a feeling of guilt, to see his coffee already poured out for him on the bedside table.

She was smiling at him in an odd sort of way, with unusual maternal tenderness.

"How are you feeling?"

He could not remember when he had last waked up with such a dreadful headache, always a sign that he had had a lot to drink. It was most unusual for him to come home tipsy. The annoying thing was that he had not even been aware that he was drinking too much. It had crept up on him, with glass after glass after glass of brandy.

"Can you remember all the things you were telling me about Aline Calas in the night?"

He preferred to forget them, having an uneasy feeling that he had grown more and more maudlin.

"You talked almost like a man in love. If I were a jealous woman . . ."

He flushed, and was at some pains to reassure her.

"I was only joking. Are you going to say all those things to Coméliau?"

So he had unburdened himself about Coméliau as well, had he? Talking to Coméliau was, in fact, the next item on the agenda—in somewhat different terms, needless to say!

"Any news, Lapointe?"

"Nothing, sir."

"I want you to get an advertisement into the afternoon edition of the newspapers. Say that the police wish to interview the young man who was given the job of depositing a suitcase at the Gare de l'Est last Sunday.

"Wasn't that Antoine?"

"I'm sure it wasn't. Pape would realize that it had much better be done by a stranger."

"The clerk says . . ."

"He saw a young man of about Antoine's age, wearing a leather jacket. That could be said of any number of young men in the district."

"Have you any proof that Pape did it?"

"He'll confess."

"Are you going to interrogate them?"

"At this stage of the proceedings, I imagine, Coméliau will be wanting to do it himself."

It was all plain sailing now, a mere matter of putting questions at random, or "fishing," as they called it among themselves.

Anyway, Maigret was not at all sure that he wanted to be the one to drive Aline Calas and Dieudonné Pape to the wall. Both would hold out to the bitter end, until it was no longer possible to remain silent.

He spent nearly an hour upstairs in the judge's office. He rang Maître Canonge from there. The telephone bell must have waked the notary with a start.

"Who's there?" he asked, in such comical bewilderment that Maigret smiled.

"Chief Superintendent Maigret."

"What time is it?"

"Half past ten. Judge Coméliau, the Examining Magistrate in charge of the case, wishes to see you in his office as soon as possible."

"Tell him I'll be right over. Shall I bring the Boissancourt papers?"

"If you will."

"I hope I didn't keep you up too late?"

The notary must have got to bed even later. God knows where he landed up after I left him, thought Maigret, hearing a woman's sleepy voice asking: "What's the time?"

Maigret returned to his office.

"Is he going to interrogate them?" Lapointe asked.

"Yes."

"Starting with the woman?"

"I advised him to start with Pape."

"Is he more likely to crack?"

"Yes. Especially as he was the one who struck Calas down, or so I believe."

"Are you going out?"

"There's something I want to clear up at the Hôtel-Dieu."

It was a small point. Lucette Calas was in the operating theater. He had to wait until the operation was over.

"I take it you've read the papers, and know of your father's death and your mother's arrest?"

"Sooner or later, something of the kind was bound to happen."

"When you last went to see her, was it to ask for money?"

"No."

"What was it, then?"

"To tell her that, as soon as he gets his divorce, Professor Lavaud and I are going to be married. He might have asked to meet my parents, and I wanted them to be presentable."

"Don't you know that Boissancourt is dead?"

"Who's he?"

She was genuinely bewildered.

"Your grandfather."

186

Casually, as though the matter were of no importance, he said:

"Unless she's convicted of murder, your mother is heir to a château, eighteen farms, and goodness only knows how many millions."

"Are you quite sure?"

"Go and see Maître Canonge, the notary, at the Hôtel d'Orsay. He's administering the estate."

"Will he be there all day?"

"I imagine so."

She did not ask what was to become of her mother. As he walked away, he gave a little shrug.

Maigret had no lunch that day. He was not hungry, but a couple of glasses of beer settled his stomach more or less. He shut himself up in his office the whole afternoon. In front of him on the desk lay the keys to the bistro in the Quai de Valmy and Pape's flat. He polished off a mass of boring administrative work, which he usually hated. Today, he seemed to be taking a perverse delight in it.

Each time the telephone rang he snatched it off the hook with uncharacteristic eagerness, but it was after five o'clock before he heard the voice of Coméliau on the line.

"Maigret?"

"Yes."

There was a note of triumph in the magistrate's voice.

"I have had them formally charged and arrested."

"All three of them?"

"No. I've released the boy Antoine."

"Have the other two confessed?"

"Yes."

"Everything?"

"Everything that *we* suspected. I decided that it

would be a good idea to start with the man. I outlined my reconstruction of the crime. He had no choice but to confess."

"What about the woman?"

"Pape repeated his admissions in her presence. It was impossible for her to deny the truth of his statement."

"Did she have anything else to say?"

"No. She just asked me, as she was leaving, whether you had seen to her cat."

"What did you say?"

"That you had better things to do."

Maigret could never forgive Judge Coméliau for that.

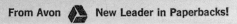
The Classic Crime Collection

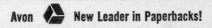

Avon 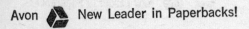 New Leader in Paperbacks!

The Startling Adventures of
THE BARON
BY

John Creasey